SEVEN TEARS INTO THE SEA

TERRI FARLEY

SIMON PULSE

NEW YORK   LONDON   TORONTO   SYDNEY

This book is a work of fiction. Any references to historical events, real people, or real locales are used fictitiously. Other names, characters, places, and incidents are the product of the author's imagination, and any resemblance to actual events or locales or persons, living or dead, is entirely coincidental.

〰〰 SIMON PULSE
An imprint of Simon & Schuster Children's Publishing Division
1230 Avenue of the Americas, New York, NY 10020
Copyright © 2005 by Terri Farley
All rights reserved, including the right of reproduction
in whole or in part in any form.
SIMON PULSE and colophon are registered
trademarks of Simon & Schuster, Inc.
Designed by Tom Daly
The text of this book was set in Zapf Calligraphic BT.
Manufactured in the United States of America
First Simon Pulse edition April 2005
10 9 8 7 6 5 4 3 2
Library of Congress Control Number 2004105857
ISBN 0-689-86442-6

To my mother, who saw worlds in tidepools and taught
her children to be comfortable in their own skins.
May your beaches be warm and endless.

Acknowledgements
Without Julia Richardson and Karen Solem, *Seven Tears into
the Sea* would have drifted away like a dream. They pronounced
magic words over my idea—"It gives me chills"—
and poof, it became a book.

MIDNIGHT

❖

MIRAGE BEACH

This is what it's like to be crazy.

All alone on the beach in the middle of the night, I'm facing huge black waves. My insides vibrate at their thunder. Even a ten-year-old knows better than to be standing here.

The soles of my feet are rock bruised from the cottage driveway that leads down to the dunes, through the sea grass, and finally to the shore.

Wind blows in my face and whips my nightgown out behind me. A storm is lurking off the coast. Hunched down, it tries to hide, but clouds cluster on its back.

Even though I see it waiting, something's making me walk through the flying sand and wind-spun fog.

Using both hands, I hold my hair away from my face. I sense someone watching me.

Part of me wants to go home, but the voice that told me to leave my bed still echoes around me. The thing it belongs to keeps me here, but I'm not afraid.

The waves rear up, then bow. Pale ruffles show at their tops, then skitter along, running to the right, farther away, and farther. Then the foam is out of sight, like the hem of a white nightgown someone snatches around a corner.

Like my white nightgown.

Crack! The waves break and slam toward me. I take a deep breath of salt air, knowing these waves won't reach me.

This is my beach. I've always lived here, and I can tell these waves aren't wild enough to drown me. Though they crash, threaten, and rush forward, they finally lay down, spreading white foam over the sand, around black rocks. Hissing a little, they hide my feet in bubbles. A strand of seaweed curls around my ankle, then flicks loose so it can float away on a wave that sucks sand from under my toes.

As the water pulls away, the sand is bare and shiny except for footprints.

They're not mine. They're ahead of me. They lead into the ocean and I have to follow them. I step in each one, and though whoever made them is bigger, the prints welcome my feet, cradling them, coaxing me to follow.

The sea's churning should have erased them, but they're still here. I look down. The waves lap at my knees. I can't see underwater, but down in the sand my toes find each footprint.

Another row of waves stands up and cracks loud as a slam-

2

ming door. The sound pulls my eyes back to the horizon, and I see him.

Moving away, darker than the night, a shadow is going out to meet the waves.

"Stop!" I hold my hands around my mouth, making a megaphone. Does he want to drown? "Come back!"

But he's diving into the heart of a wave.

Trotting through water, I fight against my nightgown, which wraps me like a mummy. My toes jam against a submerged rock and I slip. I put my arms out to catch myself, but I crash through the surface. Suddenly I'm sinking, in over my head.

Salty water stings the inside of my nose as I bob up sputtering, coughing, and still watching the ocean. He's gone. My toes stretch, trying to reach sand again.

There. Tiptoe, tiptoe. My feet touch down and I stagger to a stop and stare into the night sky.

I know you, Moon. It looks like a yellow balloon about to burst as it shines on a black cutout swimming into the storm. He's still there, but he's going to die.

I'm wishing it wouldn't happen when all at once the world turns quiet.

Waves whisper and the wind holds its breath.

A warm current swirls around me. I glance down, hoping it's not a shark.

It's nothing but my own tears striking the moon-polished water. Tears start silver ripples. I rub the tears away, then look up to see the figure stop swimming.

He's standing still. The way he's tipping his head, he seems to be listening.

"Come back!" I yell so hard it's like when you skin your knee, only this time it feels like I've skinned my throat.

And he turns around! My heart's jumping. Then, all at once, the man, sky, and beach are blotted out by a black wave.

It slaps me flat. I feel my hair spreading out like a mermaid's. I blink into darkness.

A night bird dives so low I hear feathers rustle, but that's not what wakes me.

An arm works under me, between my shoulders and the sand, lifting.

I'm still on the beach, feeling dizzy. I never should have left my bed. You have to be careful when something in the dark is calling your name.

I'm sitting up when a hand brushes sand from my cheek.

"Mom—?"

But when my eyes open, moonlight shows me a Gypsy. Right there. Next to me, close enough that I smell wind and salt water on his shoulders. Wet black hair curves in thorn shapes around slightly tilted eyes.

Careful, I tell myself. He's a stranger.

I draw a breath to ask why he'd walked out into the ocean and isn't he sorry for getting me pounded against the rocks? Instead, I gag and press my hands over my mouth to keep *from throwing up the saltwater I had swallowed.*

Standing might help, so I push with my wobbly legs and he does the rest, rising with me, steadying my arm, smiling.

Joy bounds up in me. I must know him. He must be a friend. I must recognize that grin, because even though he doesn't say anything, I feel him telling me you're okay.

Then everything goes crazy. A siren wails. His grip loosens.

I don't blame him for wanting to escape, but my mouth is saying, "Don't go."

He doesn't.

He holds me close to his side. He's tall, and that doesn't scare me, but he's naked, and I know he shouldn't be. For one more second his warm arm circles my shoulders, the way a bird shelters babies under its wing.

Against my ear he whispers words I don't know.

When he pulls away, my wet nightgown sticks to his arm. And then he goes, leaving me, but still hesitating at the water's edge.

The rasping tires of a police car lurch off the highway, crunching over the gravel. A car door slams.

The Gypsy should run, but he doesn't. He's ready to return to the waves, but still he's looking back at me.

The moonlight's so bright I can see him lick his lips. Then he tries to talk, frowning to get the words right.

"Beckon the sea, I'll come to thee . . .

"Shed seven tears, perchance seven years."

Shouts are coming closer. I look up the hill and see flashlight beams bobbing.

When I turn back to face him, he's gone.

My head swings from side to side. I look up the shore, then back to the waves. I look up at the cottage, then out to sea.

He's just not there.

I hear the quiet lap of sea on stone, but even the waves are empty. The Gypsy boy is gone, and I stand on the beach, alone.

CHAPTER ONE

❖

SEVEN YEARS LATER

The VW took the curve fast.

Wind blasted through my hair, waving it in front of my eyes before snatching it straight behind me.

"Faster!" Mandi cheered from the backseat.

I gripped the steering wheel and pressed the gas pedal just a little. The VW was my seventeenth birthday present, and I wasn't completely used to it yet. Besides, this two-lane coastal highway kept swooping around turns. What if I came face-to-face with some car passing another car? I'd rather not do that at full speed, since I'd have to pull over against the rock cliff and risk scuffing up my Bug.

It wasn't a brand new Bug, but it was a convertible,

and my folks had paid for a fresh paint job. "Arrest-me yellow," Dad called the color I'd picked, but he didn't say no. Two of my aunts had chipped in to help me buy a sound system that can blast your spine back into the new seat covers.

I loved my car, and its maiden road trip had been perfect, even though my two best friends would be returning home without me.

I glanced up to check my rearview mirror. Dad's car was back there, somewhere. He was following with my stuff and Gumbo, my cat. Most of what I saw in my mirror was Mandi's up-jutting thumb, still urging me to go faster.

I shook my head because I didn't want Dad lecturing me on speeding the minute we arrived at Mirage Beach. Beside me, Jill nodded her support.

"You guys," Mandi leaned against the back of my seat, shouting next to my ear so I'd hear her over the wind. "Did you see the *men*, in that green truck?"

"You mean the thugs we saw back in that little town?" Jill raised one thin black eyebrow, then shouted, "Watch out!"

I swerved to avoid a swathe of broken glass glittering across my lane and missed most of it.

Keep your eyes on the road, I told myself. *We're almost there.*

"They're cute thugs, at least the blond one," Mandi insisted. "Besides . . ."

I could hear her working into scolding mode, and I smiled.

"Think of Belle and her Beast—"

Really, even though she's going to be a senior, Mandi has swallowed the whole fairy-tale-prince myth. Jill pretended to bang her head against the window as Mandi continued.

"—sometimes you just don't know what's under that scruffy exterior."

Mandi's fatal flaw was that she'd investigate way too many Beasts if Jill and I didn't keep her straight. This summer, Jill would have to handle the job alone.

It turned out to be a good thing that I hadn't gone faster. Not because of the guys, but because suddenly, down to our left, the cove appeared. Gold sand, black rocks, and turquoise water materialized. The sight took our breaths away. Even mine.

Up to our right, above it all, sat the Sea Horse Inn, perched like a wedding cake on the bluff overlooking the sea.

"Wow," Jill said. "Gwen, you had me feeling sorry for you because you'd be without us, but this is incredible."

"Like Tahiti or something," Mandi agreed.

"I can't believe you never come here," Jill said. "And that"—she tapped the windshield—"is Cook's Cottage, right? Your family's place? And you'll have it all to yourself. *Such* possibilities, you lucky girl."

"That's me."

As a child I'd thought the whitewashed cottage looked like an ugly duckling squatting beside the swan-like inn. Since then, I'd been living in Valencia, a San Francisco suburb, where each house looked pretty much like its neighbor. Now I realized the cottage was cute.

But I'd sworn never to come back. *Never* should last longer than seven years.

"Just like playing house," I joked to smother the dark thoughts roiling around in my mind. My cheeks felt hot, nerves cranked tight inside my chest, and I couldn't keep the whispered gossip from replaying.

"*. . . heard about the incident at the cove . . .*"

"*Gwennie Cook was walking in her sleep, I heard and almost fell from Mirage Point . . .*"

"*That's what they're saying, of course . . .*"

"*. . . moving? After what, three generations at the Point?*"

"*She says a naked man just materialized from the waves and vanished back into them. She became absolutely hysterical when the police questioned her . . .*"

"*You don't think . . . ?*"

If I'd just agreed I was sleepwalking, everything would have been fine. No scandal, no ugly suspicions. But I remembered shouting and stamping, insisting I hadn't been alone.

Small towns never forget. Just read Stephen King or watch a Western where a gunslinger tries to go straight.

As soon as the people in town saw me, they'd be gossiping. If Nana hadn't maintained I was the one she needed, I wouldn't be here.

I slid my hand over the steering wheel, downshifted, and took the off-ramp with calm skill, even though the memories made me angry.

Ten-year-olds aren't stupid. I could remember being in the grocery store and hearing hushed voices filter past the canned goods on the next aisle. I'd peered through and saw women with their heads together, talking about me. When I marched around the end of the aisle and faced them, chin up, fisted hands shaking, they'd just smiled sympathetic smiles.

Maybe they really were sympathetic. It was the first time I had heard my name in the same sentence as the word "molested."

I knew I hadn't been molested, but my memories of Mirage Point were a mixture of fantasy and reality.

I drew a breath so deep the seat belt tightened across my chest. If there was one thing I was determined to do this summer, it was find out what had really happened that night on the beach.

Distracted, I'd driven right past the gravel road to the cottage.

"We'll just check out the Inn and say 'hi' to my grandmother," I said, as if that had been my plan all along.

Almost at once, I spotted the lip of a freshly blacktopped

driveway. I turned, surprised how steep it was, swooping from the street to the Sea Horse Inn.

I did want to see Nana. My grandmother is my role model.

Nana is stubborn, strong-minded, and pretty frisky for a seventy-year-old. To tell the truth, I was surprised she'd admitted needing help. If she hadn't actually broken her leg in the accident, I'd think she was up to something.

After all, she had Thelma, who'd been at the Inn forever to clean and do laundry.

But three weeks ago, Nana had called Dad and claimed she needed another pair of hands to help serve breakfast and afternoon tea, and those hands had to be mine.

Once I got over being flattered, I told Mom and Dad no. I love Nana, but I didn't want to leave my friends and my summer job. Not that I'd gone out and found one yet, but they knew I needed money. I never have the right clothes for anything. I end up borrowing Mandi's—which they say are too tight.

But my parents didn't give me a choice. I was staying at Mirage Beach all summer.

My parents are so inconsistent, they make me crazy. When I turned twelve, they started talking back to the television. Those announcements would flash on, with the audio saying, "It's 10 P.M., do you know where your children are?" and they'd answer.

I'm not allowed to go anywhere without first getting lectures on kidnapping, date rape, and drunk drivers. I'm not as naive as they think. I know those things happen, and I'm careful. But that's not good enough for them.

Even if I only want to go to a friend's house to watch videos, my parents call to make sure there'll be an adult around. It's humiliating.

It's especially bad, because Jill is totally free. After ten years in foster care, she petitioned the court to make her an emancipated minor.

Mandi's dad is more like my parents. Intermittently.

And yet, despite their paranoia, my parents had decreed I must go live in Cook's Cottage. All summer, all alone.

"We're here." I yanked on the emergency brake.

Even though Mandi was pushing her shoulder, hurrying her, Jill tucked her black Cleopatra hair behind her ears before extracting herself from the backseat.

Mandi was right behind her. They began oohing at the stone maiden pouring water into the goldfish pond and aahing at the stained-glass oval hanging from the Inn's rafters. It spun in the breeze as sunlight struck emerald, gold, and aqua beams from the mosaic sea horse in its center.

As we started up to the wide veranda, I skipped steps and breathed in the scent of Nana's violets and roses. Halfway up, I felt the strongest urge to jog straight through the house, over the back lawn, and down the path that led to the cove.

I remembered the cove as a neat scoop of turquoise water studded with black rocks and sea lions. There was a stone arch there too, and a mysterious grotto. Hidden from the Inn, it was a secret world. Jill and Mandi would go nuts for it. But the trail down was wet, narrow, and risky. You couldn't rush.

I almost ran into Mandi as she stopped on the top step and swiveled around, hands on hips.

Overhead, the stained-glass sea horse spun faster. It used to be Dad's job to unhook it from the rafters and bring it inside when the weather turned stormy.

Mandi tugged the hem of her backless magenta top and surveyed the wide green lawns.

"What a great party house!" Mandi said. "It'd be awesome if you had everybody up at the end of summer."

The idea made me uneasy. Through the Inn's open front door came a faint bustle of conversation, clinking silverware, and a fluting melody. Everything about the Inn said good manners and quiet afternoons, not hip-hop with the bass turned to a deafening throb.

16

"Maybe," I said, even though I wasn't a fan of huge parties, and I wanted to keep a low profile in Mirage Beach.

Over Mandi's head Jill gave me her standard sarcastic smile. She didn't think much of Mandi's idea, but she kept quiet because I had.

I am the glue keeping the two of them together. Jill works forty hours a week through a work-study program her counselor helped set up. Almost every dollar of Jill's earnings go to pay for rent and food. She earns a 4.0 every semester, and she's determined to become a professional singer. she'll do it, too. Maybe because she had a really scummy childhood, she's driven to be successful.

Mandi's definition of success is different. She's rich, ditzy, and all wound up with finding Prince Charming. It's probably because her dad is too busy for her. Jill and I have pointed this out to her, in a nice way, but she just feels sorry for us because we lack romantic souls.

Summer at Mirage Beach would have been a lot more fun if Jill and Mandi could have stayed with me. That had been our plan until Jill landed her dream job and Mandi got an offer she couldn't refuse.

I understood, but grudgingly.

And then, I didn't have time to mope.

"Come hug me!" Nana stood framed in the doorway.

She wasn't your everyday grandma. Her tea-colored hair curved in a million directions. She wore hippieish clothes: gold hoop earrings and a peasant blouse over a long patchwork skirt. She only wobbled a little as she crossed the threshold to hug me.

Nana still smelled of baby powder and bread dough, but our heads nuzzled into the sides of each other's necks. We were the same height and that was really weird. Had I grown that much since I left here?

"A bigger hug," Nana ordered. "My ribs are healed. It's only this leg giving me trouble."

Even though I could feel Jill and Mandi watching, I put up with the public display because Nana felt frail. She'd always been a tall, striding woman. Now her shoulders felt fragile as bird bones. It was a good thing I'd come to Sea Horse Inn.

Before shutting the door, Nana glanced down the road for Dad, gave a little shrug, then we went inside.

I could tell Jill and Mandi were stunned by the inn's beauty.

So was I. As a little girl, I'd arranged my plastic farm animals under that polished mahogany piano. I'd bumped on my bottom down every step in that dramatic staircase. During my skateboard stage, I'd crashed into that antique sideboard, which held a crystal bowl of shells and fresh flowers.

The smell of beeswax candles and the ocean views out each window filled me up and made me sigh. This was my grandmother's house. Mirage Beach was my second home, and I was too mature, now, to let one night ruin it for me.

Mandi tried not to act impressed. Her dad has brought home three new stepmothers since her mom left, and he's remodeled their house for each one, so Mandi is used to nice things.

Now she was tossing her honey-colored hair and frowning toward the ceiling as footsteps crossed overhead. It could be guests or Thelma making beds.

"I don't suppose the Inn is haunted," Mandi joked.

Even though it wasn't funny, I laughed a little because the truth was, Thelma had haunted me a little bit. The prospect of seeing her again worried me. She was the one who'd reported the incident on the beach when I was ten. What she'd told the police, that night, was different from what I'd told them. Because I was a little kid, of course they had believed her.

Sourness gathered at the back of my throat when I thought about facing Thelma, but that would come later.

Nana liked Jill. I could see it in the way she shook Jill's hand and smiled at her.

Before Nana could greet Mandi, Dad came whooshing in. He moved around Nana's kitchen, shutting a drawer and pushing down the flipped-up edge of a throw rug, in a way that told you he'd grown up in this house. It also underlined his belief that a kitchen was the most dangerous room in any house.

I mean, everyone's careful with knives and electrical cords, but Dad could tell you which evil particles linger in the air after frying a chicken and which bacteria cling to a freshly mopped floor just waiting to ambush crawling babies. Don't get him started on the pollution properties of air freshener.

Dad was a broad-shouldered geek. That's how Mom described the man she'd married when they both were in college. He'd always been cautious. Becoming a moderately successful mystery writer had only made him worse.

Now he was watching Nana and searching for hazards.

"Mother, should you be up?" He used a tone that I'd get grounded for, but Nana brushed it off.

"I'm not an invalid. They call this a walking cast"—Nana pulled her skirt aside to rap on her white plaster-encased leg—"for a reason."

Dad shook his head. As if he wanted backup, he turned to Jill and Mandi. "Did Gwen tell you about my mom? She was taking drinks—"

"Apple cider," Nana clarified.

"—up to guests watching migrating whales from the widow's walk."

"That little balcony thing on top of the house," I explained when Mandi frowned in confusion. Again.

"Sea captains' wives used to go up to keep watch for their husbands' ships."

"Of course," Jill said, nodding. Then with a perfectly straight face, she turned to Mandi and added, "I think there was one in *The Little Mermaid*."

"Really?" Mandi asked, but her face lit up.

"Mom was wearing one of her oddball outfits," Dad went on, gesturing at Nana's skirt, "and she tripped down the stairs. Broke two ribs and her right leg. It's a wonder she hasn't done it before now."

"It's a wonder you don't turn into a clucking hen, the way you worry." Nana shook her head and patted Dad's cheek.

Nana had nailed it. Dad was psychotic about safety. Mom blamed (when Dad was out of the room, of course) the books he wrote. Dad is Jeffery Cook, author of the Scratch Boiselle books, about this New Orleans detective who's always uncovering voodoo cults, getting mugged on Bourbon Street, and getting locked in crypts. Looking for danger in unexpected places is what Dad gets paid for.

That was okay in fiction, even kind of okay when he was watching over me. But he was talking to his mother. Nana had taken care of herself for a long time. Anyone could have an accident.

Dad jammed his hands into his pockets and jingled his car keys. "Let's get you settled, shall we? And introduce Gumbo to her new digs?" Dad gestured toward the front of the Inn, where he'd parked. "The way she's been yowling inside her carrier, she may have deafened herself. I know she made a good start on me."

"Poor kitty," I said. My calico cat deserved better. She was the only roommate who'd stayed with the plan to spend the summer at the cottage. Then again, she *had* come in a cage.

"You have plenty of time to get settled and be back in time for tea," Nana said.

When Nana said "tea," she didn't mean what most people did. The Sea Horse Inn served a north-coast version of a proper English tea. It was given a four star rating in tourist guidebooks. Now that vacation season was in full swing, she'd need my help to do things like arrange scones on platters, swirl Devonshire cream around raspberries, and pour tea from heavy sterling pots.

It was one of the best things about the Inn, but when Mandi and Jill tensed up and looked at me, I knew they weren't tempted to stay.

"It'll just be me, Nana," I said.

"Oh no!" Nana's eyes and mouth widened in disappointment. "I knew your friends had decided against staying the summer, but I'd hoped they'd be here for tea."

Jill smoothed her hair, and her eyes shone with that high intensity concern they get when she thinks her reputation is on the line.

"I'm sorry," Jill said before I could make an excuse. "I

have to work tonight. And most of the summer. I'm banking everything I can for college tuition. My first payment is only a year away."

I noticed Jill didn't mention she was waiting tables at the Torch, a forties-style cabaret, so that she could have a chance at the stage during band breaks. That was the real reason she'd taken the job. So she could sing. But Jill was cautious, in case Nana thought it was an inappropriate job for a high school girl.

"We'll miss Gwen. And Mirage Beach is incredible," Jill added. "I could get addicted to this place."

"It does have a way of stealing your heart," Nana admitted.

Something in my chest trembled at that, but it felt more like fear than affection. What was that about?

"Mrs. Cook?"

Of course Mandi used Nana's name. Memorizing names was her hobby. She believed knowing the names of every student at Valencia High would guarantee her election as Homecoming Queen next year. She hoped to have Prince Charming on her arm by then. If not, it was still a step in the right direction.

"I'm sorry, too. I have a new stepmother, and this one came with *twins* who need an in-house baby-sitter. So my dad's keeping me on a short leash this summer."

"My goodness, dear," Nana said. "I certainly understand."

I couldn't help sliding Mandi a look out of the corner of my eye. She'd left out the part where she'd get a new BMW in September if she chauffeured the twins around to tennis and swimming lessons all summer.

The BMW was bound to be Prince bait, but Mandi's face turned solemn as she added, "My father thinks the responsibility will be good for me."

"I'll be back soon, Mom, for a longer visit." Dad kissed Nana's cheek as we moved out of the kitchen. "I'll just check things at the cottage, get Gwennie settled, then whisk these working girls back to the city."

"Thelma's washed the curtains, swept, put fresh linens on the bed, all that," Nana told him at the door.

"It'll be real nice," Dad said, but he was already climbing into the Honda.

"You might make sure the extra key is where it's supposed to be," Nana called after him, and Dad flashed her an okay sign over the roof of his car.

Jill and Mandi were ahead of me, piling back into the VW when I felt that pull toward the ocean, again.

"Beckon the sea, I'll come to thee . . ."

No. I actually shook my head to keep the words from taking root. I'd picked up that rhyme from some Celtic story Nana told. Not from a stranger on the beach.

"Shed seven tears, perchance seven years."

It was coincidence that I hadn't been back to Mirage Beach for seven years. Pure coincidence, and I was not about to go stand in the waves and squeeze out seven tears.

The image was embarrassing, not scary. So why, though it had to be eighty degrees, was I rubbing goose-flesh from my arms?

Nana's sigh made me look back. She was gazing after Dad.

"As old as I am," she said, when she caught me watching. "I still haven't got used to the idea that he's mostly your father now, instead of my son."

It was an incredibly sad thing to say.

For a minute I didn't know how to react. Then I decided it was a reminder of how quickly time passed. It had been years since I spent time with Nana, and all because I was afraid of gossip.

I darted back up the steps and gave Nana a quick kiss on the cheek.

"The minute I get rid of them, I'll be back," I promised. "Will you save me a couple scones?"

"All you want, Gwennie," Nana promised. "And a private moment"—she raised one eyebrow—"after things settle down?"

Oh no. I knew what was coming.

I also knew I couldn't get out of it.

I nodded, waved, and sprinted toward the VW. Mandi and Jill were settled in the car, and I was glad their impatience had kept them from hearing Nana's invitation.

I started the car and revved the engine.

A sea gull cried and swooped so low that all three of us ducked, then laughed.

Driving like a pro, I pulled out of the driveway, speeding after Dad.

This is really why I didn't want to come back. I could get past the gossip. I'd outgrown the sleepwalking. But what about Nana's totally goofy predictions?

I'm a person who can't take a weather forecast on faith, and Nana expected me to believe she could see my future reflected in an antique copper mirror.

It's like carnival fortune-tellers reading crystal balls, and it's called scrying. It turns up in lots of old stories. In *Snow White*, for instance, when the evil queen says "Mirror, mirror on the wall," then gets answers from that mirror, she's scrying.

Oh my gosh, Mandi had me doing it, too.

Snow White is a fairy tale, I reminded myself. I live in this century, in the real world. I don't believe in scrying.

I lifted my chin, squared my shoulders, and watched the road.

Dad turned hard right, down the dirt road to Cook's Cottage, and I followed.

"We are gonna have such awesome tans by September," Mandi squealed. She thrust her arms toward the sky, and I knew how she felt.

Ahead, waves rumbled. Sea wind rushed into my face. I smelled salt, kelp, and sunbaked tar paper on the cottage roof. Summer was making lots of promises.

"I propose a party at my apartment, the night before school starts," Jill said. "To tell our summer stories."

"And compare tan lines!" Mandi said. She craned her neck and peeled down one side of her blouse to inspect her starting point.

"And don't forget our promise," I reminded them.

"Sure, it will be easy for you to try something new every day," Mandi said, pretending to pout.

"I'm sure the twins will give you a few thrills and surprises," I answered, but I was actually thinking it might be fun to let Nana read my future. She hadn't done it since we left Mirage Beach.

That last day as Mom and I waited for Dad to return with the U-Haul trailer that would carry everything we owned to Valencia, Nana had plucked the copper mirror out of its pouch and insisted on doing a reading.

Mom had resisted. Before she became a health writer at the *Valencia View* newspaper, Mom was a nurse. She has a scientific brain, so Nana's scrying made Mom crazy.

"Now, now," Nana had soothed Mom as she fidgeted at Nana's kitchen window, mumbling that Dad had better get back and break up this séance, "this will be a true reading. I can feel it in my bones."

The gist of the reading was that I'd return to Mirage Beach. That was a pretty safe call, since we wouldn't desert Nana, and she knew it. But one part of the reading really stuck with me.

I think it would have anyway, but Mom guaranteed it when she yelped, "Why on earth would you say something like that to a *child*?"

Nana had stared at the copper circle cupped in her palm, and though she was seated right next to me, her eyes saw things far beyond the kitchen table.

"The power which commands the waves, will pull you back," she whispered. "Back to a reunion no mortal can imagine and no female can resist."

To forget words like those, you'd have to be brain-dead.

CHAPTER TWO

❖

A bird's nest hung between the door hinge and the eaves of Cook's Cottage. I noticed it just as Mandi started to jerk open the screen door.

"Wait!" I said, and though the little mud pellets, all stuck together to make a gourd-shaped nest, shuddered, they didn't fall apart.

"It's a wasp's nest," Jill said. "There must be something around here we can knock it down with."

"It's not a wasp's nest, is it, Dad?" I turned to my father as Jill crossed her arms.

Jill isn't as softhearted over animals as I am. Even though her landlord allows small pets, she doesn't have one. She says she has enough trouble feeding herself.

"Cliff swallows," Dad said. He pushed his glasses

up his nose and stood listening to the nest.

"Can you see inside?" I asked. "Are there any eggs?"

"I don't want to look in with my giant face and scare them." Dad shook his head and backed away, lowering his voice as if he'd wake the occupants. "I didn't see anybody fly away, but we used to have them every year."

"If they're *cliff* swallows, wouldn't it be for their own good to—" Mandi made a sweeping gesture over her head, then shifted her weight toward Jill. "I bet they'd be happier down by the cliffs."

The nest did look like someone had just slung a clump of mud on the cottage wall. And it would be in danger each time my front door opened. And Gumbo's hunting hum was already coming from her cage. I could picture her with head cocked at the door, alert for the sounds of nestlings taking wing for the first time. Still, I wanted to leave the nest right where it was.

"Haven't you heard of the famous swallows of San Juan Capistrano?"

I hated it when Dad asked my friends questions like that. Of course they hadn't. This time he recognized my frustration, because he went on as if they'd answered.

"They've been coming back to a mission for generations, since, oh, I don't know, the 1800s, I think. It's swallows' nature to find a home and stick with it."

Jill, Mandi, and Dad watched me for a decision.

"They stay," I told them, and the zing of possessiveness felt good.

Then I held my screen door wide, while Dad reached through to unlock the wooden door and ease inside.

"I've never seen the Nature Girl side of you, Gwen," Jill said.

"It's going to look like crap until it dries up and falls off," Mandi warned.

But she followed Jill, eager as I was to see inside Cook's Cottage, and it occurred to me that they both might be just a little bit jealous.

Inside, the cottage seemed smaller than I remembered. I suppose that was because I'd been pretty little when I lived here.

"I love this place," Jill said. "It's so light."

Jill's studio sat in a hive of identical apartments shadowed by a freeway overpass, so I understood her admiration, but the truth was, the cottage was much brighter than I recalled.

The curtains were pushed back from each window. June light streamed across the plank floors of golden oak. Except where they were covered by sea grass rugs, they were smooth and glossy.

The cottage had four rooms. Downstairs, there was the living room, a kitchen, and my bedroom. From where I stood by the front door, I could see the staircase leading up to the sleeping loft my parents had shared.

Every wall in the place was painted white and the windows had pale gauzy curtains. I'm surprised Dad wasn't fussing about them being transparent.

The couch was adobe-colored, faded but not ratty. I could very clearly see myself lounging with a book and a can of soda. My sandy beach towel would be draped over a chair pulled up to the round kitchen table. My curtains would billow like sails, and I could hear my seashell wind chimes tinkling in the breeze.

Of course, there weren't any wind chimes in the window or beach towels yet. And, far from fussing about my thin curtains, Dad was chuckling with pleasure because Cook's Cottage still had a dead bolt on the front door and latches on the windows.

Was he thinking of keeping me in or keeping trouble out?

I carried Gumbo's cage and followed Dad on his inspection tour. Mandi and Jill were right behind me.

When Gumbo gave a throaty growl, I peered in at her usually good-natured calico face. Her ears were pressed flat and the gold of her eyes barely showed through the angry slits.

"Had enough, baby?" I asked, then hid her carrier behind the couch, where it would be relatively quiet. As soon as it was just the two of us, I'd let her out to explore.

Dad paused in his scrutiny, hands in pockets. He

nodded to himself, as if this just might do for his daughter. Then he continued walking around, checking lamp cords for frays, sniffing the burners on the gas stove, shouldering a tall bookcase full of old hardbacks to see if it would topple in an earthquake.

"Looks like I'm safe from everything but paper cuts," I teased.

"I'd be happier if there was a phone, but you're only a two-minute sprint from the Inn," he muttered.

"No phone?" Mandi gasped as if he'd said there was no oxygen. "What will you do?"

"Use the one at the Inn," I said, and because I could see she was about to resurrect the cell phone issue, I shook my head.

Dad had read that you could spontaneously combust if you used a cell phone while pumping gasoline. Now that I had a car of my own, he found this to be a serious concern.

I had forgotten the no-phone part of living at the cottage, but I wasn't freaked out about it.

I flicked the light switch beside the door. A porch light, pale in the sunshine, came on. At least I had electricity. I wondered if the birds had built there because the porch light kept them warm.

Of course that was unlikely, since no one lived here.

"Don't forget where these are." Dad opened a

kitchen cabinet full of candles and held up a box of matches. "You probably don't remember that whenever there's a storm, nine times out of ten it knocks out the power."

I remembered candles flickering all around me. From the mantle, the coffee table, everywhere. I remembered picnic dinners of salami and cheese and French bread and butter on a blanket in front of the fireplace, and the three of us going to bed at the same time instead of Mom and Dad staying up late.

"Power failures were fun," I told him. Dad's musing expression said he remembered too.

"They were," he admitted. "But if you have one this summer, hightail it over to the Inn. Mom still doesn't have a generator, but they're set up for living in the 1800s."

Jill and Mandi stood close together, looking bored and a little unsure of me. I'd totally ignored them for about ten minutes.

"Make yourselves at home. Explore," I encouraged them. "Investigate."

With a shrug and a smile, Mandi headed for the refrigerator and swung the door open wide.

"Oh yeah, this is what I'm talking about!" She grabbed a soda, passed one to me, then Jill, and began reading neatly labeled containers. "Four-cheese ravioli, yum. Ginger carrots—"

"Sounds good," Jill mused.

"Oh wait," Mandi brandished a foil-wrapped package, "Upsy-daisy donut loaf!"

My friends moved on to the cupboards. They were fully stocked too. More evidence Nana and Thelma had really gotten into the playhouse spirit.

Gripping the diet cola as if it could fortify me, I moved stiffly to the doorway of my old bedroom.

It wasn't much bigger than the inside of my VW, so my two suitcases took up most of the floor space not occupied by my childhood bike, which leaned against one wall, and the bed.

A purple spread stitched with multicolored wildflowers covered the bed, and a full-length mirror hung on the wall. A shelf held a collection of shells and sand dollars, and the window had extra latches.

I must have had years of peaceful sleep in here, but I wondered if that mirror still held nighttime images of me lying on that bed, spine pressed into the mattress, fists clenched, eyes burning as I stared at the ceiling, trying to stay awake.

I remembered fighting drowsiness because I didn't know where I'd wake up.

"You could sleep in the loft," Dad offered.

I jumped, unaware he'd stood behind me as I braced in the doorway.

"Really?" I said. "I can?"

"Why not?" Dad dipped his arm in a be-my-guest motion.

"You guys!" I shouted to Jill and Mandi. "Come with me!"

I ran up the stairs and they pounded after me. Like kindergartners, we leaped onto the king-size bed in the center of the loft. We looked left, out the triangular window fitted under the eaves, and saw my car in the driveway and the graveled path that led to the beach. We looked right, through another triangular window, and saw the Inn and the trail to the bluff.

Straight ahead, we looked out to sea.

"Oh Gwen, you'll see the fog coming in and sailboats," Jill sighed.

Far out on the horizon, a white sail headed south for Siena Bay. Closer to Mirage Point, something black moved in the water. Someone was swimming. Out too deep. My heartbeat pounded so hard that I felt its echo in my wrists. I hadn't seen a swimmer so far out since that night.

When the swimmer vanished and didn't reappear, I knew what I'd really seen.

"It's a sea lion," I said, pointing.

Jill nodded. "This is too cool."

Mandi, however, wasn't feeling the sea's hypnotic spell.

"Kissing fish," she cooed. "What a cute bedspread."

It was, too. I'd always loved my parents' kissing fish bedspread. It was weird they'd left it behind. In the days after we moved to Valencia, I'd missed the beach and this quilt might have comforted me.

Mom and Dad always said we left Mirage Beach because Mom's job offer at the newspaper was too good to refuse. I knew that wasn't the only reason. But what was their hurry?

When it was time for everyone to leave, I discovered I'd already grown protective of my swallows' nest.

"Careful," I said, looking up toward the eaves. It wasn't like the door would hit the nest, but I was afraid a good slam would dislodge those little mud pellets.

My father and my friends squeezed through obediently, and once we were outside, hugs came from all sides. Mandi's, as I stepped off the front porch, was more like a tackle.

"I'll be back," she promised. "They'll have to give me time off from the twins. And since there's nothing to do here, you'll need me. We'll lay in the sun and talk trash about Jill."

Mandi knew I hated gossip, but she was only trying to get a rise out of Jill, and it worked.

"Hey!" Jill protested, elbowing Mandi out of the way.

"I guess you'll just have to come with me, then," she

taunted, then gave me one more squeeze and made way for Jill.

I could tell by her determined expression that Jill was thinking about "the incident." I'd told her, but not Mandi.

Since Jill had a childhood full of secrets, I'd told her mine.

With one arm around my neck, Jill caught me close enough to whisper.

"You're tough. The first busybody who stirs up that old gossip—just spit in her eye. Metaphorically speaking, of course. That'll slow down the rest of them. Besides," she said, pulling back, "you've landed in paradise."

Dad fell in beside me as we walked down to the cars.

"When you leave to go anywhere, even down to the beach or over to the Inn, lock up." He glanced at me, sideways, to make sure I was nodding. "If it rains, check the ceiling for leaks. If it is leaking, just put a pan under it and let Nana know so she can get it repaired."

"Got it," I said.

"The Bug should be fine," he continued. "But you need to drive it to keep the oil stirred up. Keep the gas tank full, and check the tire pressure whenever you think of it. And if it starts making funny noises, Jack Cates, in town, can help you out."

I could not believe Dad had suggested that Dr.

Cates—the guy who'd psychoanalyzed me when I was ten—should fix my Volkswagen.

"Don't bristle, Gwen," Dad said sharply. "He's an even better mechanic than he is a psychologist. I mean—"

That struck me funny, and I laughed until I saw Dad wanted to get into a discussion of the dark recesses of my mind. I held up a hand for him to halt and gave him a pleading look. Dad took the hint.

The minute it looked like he was really leaving, I felt like crying.

"You'll do great, Gwennie. Helping Nana this way is the most unselfish thing you've ever done. I'm proud of you."

He kissed my cheek, climbed in his car, slammed the door harder than usual, then drove away.

Mandi and Jill waved out the back window. Their hands were a blur when the car turned back onto the highway and my everyday life drove away, leaving me behind.

Freedom.

I didn't feel lonely, deserted, or scared as I walked back to Cook's Cottage. *My* cottage.

I picked a berry from the blackberry hedge that marked the boundary of a little grassy yard around Cook's Cottage. I popped the berry in my mouth, and a sour pain stabbed the tender glands behind my earlobes. I didn't care. For the summer they were my berries, and I'd decide when they were ripe.

I eased open the screen door, slipped through, and danced into the living room, singing. I shook my hips, tossed my hair, and pointed ecstatic index fingers right, left, right, left, toward heaven. I freed Gumbo from her cage too, but she rushed under the couch, obviously not in the mood for dancing.

"Perhaps we'll split a can of tuna later. 'Kay, girl-friend?" I told her, then continued my celebration by clicking on my stereo.

I'd just kicked off my sandals in exultation when I heard a creak. Then my door rattled under a stern knock.

The door has a little four-paned window at eye level. At once I recognized my visitor as Thelma.

I turned off the music.

The celebration stopped.

I opened the door. After not seeing her for years, I should have come up with something better, but all I said was, "Hi."

Thelma is built like a small refrigerator. She wears bobby socks and tennis shoes, thick-lensed glasses, and her hair—threaded by gray, now—is caught in a pony-tail bound by a green rubber band. She's always used a rubber band. She must have split ends up to her scalp.

"It's good to see you again," I managed, but I shouldn't have bothered.

"Missed your dad, did I?" Thelma's first words reminded me that some of the old folks on the coast sound sort of foreign. They don't have accents, exactly, but their English has a Celtic rhythm. Probably because the original settlers here were British.

"*Just* missed him," I agreed.

"Leaving you here alone."

I heard cars pass on the highway. From the direction of the Point, a sea lion barked. The sound of it echoed around the cove, and I really wanted to go down there.

Thelma had underlined the fact that I'd be by myself. What did that mean? Was she worried I'd go sleepwalking? A sick feeling fizzed up in my throat again.

"Well, not all alone," I told her. "I have my cat."

And then I realized I was still looking at her through the screen door.

"Sorry," I said. "Come on in."

"I'll take care not to disturb the nest," she said. "Hope you don't mind me leaving it."

"Of course not." I stopped short of saying the swallows would be company. That sounded kind of pitiful after her remark about Dad leaving me all alone.

I smooched toward the empty room behind me. "Gumbo, where are you, kitty?"

In the contrary way of cats, Gumbo didn't flick a whisker to show she was there.

"Would you like to come in? Does Nana need help doing tea?" I asked, finally taking the hint from her sudden appearance.

"New guests showed up, so there's extra work," Thelma said, then shifted her attention over my shoulder. "Was everything as it should be? Nothing mussed or out of place?"

"I haven't really—"

"You can arrange things to suit you, of course. The kitchen, for instance."

"It looks great," I assured her. "I don't cook much, though, and I've sure never had my own kitchen."

She smiled. "It's a treat. You'll be wanting to go to town for some things, won't you?" Her eyes turned watchful again.

I hesitated. It would take a little nerve to go into Siena Bay for the first time, but I only shrugged.

She glanced at her watch, and I scanned the kitchen for a clock.

"Give me a minute to change," I said, and her nod of satisfaction told me I'd made the right move.

Leaving the cottage, I noticed two things: a spider spinning her web in my blackberry bush and a wet footprint on the deck, which formed a U around three sides of the cottage.

I don't know what made me glance in the direction of my old bedroom window, but there it was. The print of a bare foot.

Since Thelma wore those black canvas numbers, and I hadn't been in the water, it was kind of unsettling.

"She'll be so glad to have you at the Inn," Thelma said, and then she took off striding, and I had to hurry to keep up.

I glanced over my shoulder as I moved away from the cottage.

Since there wasn't time to take a good look at it, I thought, following Thelma, *maybe it was something else entirely.*

So I didn't say anything about the footprint, though it would have been something to talk about.

I didn't know what to say to Thelma. She'd been the one who watched from the widow's walk at Sea Horse Inn, then called 911. If she hadn't, no one would have known about my sleepwalking and the man on the beach.

I tried not to hold a grudge. No doubt, Thelma believed she'd done a good deed. Most people thought she'd rescued me. I didn't see it that way then, and I still don't. If she hadn't made that phone call, I probably would have awakened from my dream and scampered back home. I wouldn't be returning to Mirage Beach now, uncertain as I was seven years ago.

❖ ❖ ❖

The present overcame the past, big time, the moment I walked through the kitchen door of the Sea Horse Inn. Earlier in the afternoon when I'd been here with Dad and my friends, it had felt like a normal—if big and well-equipped—family kitchen. Now, just thirty minutes before tea was to be served to paying guests, I was surrounded by a whir of business.

It was a safe bet that I couldn't get my fortune read from the copper mirror for at least a few hours.

A dozen or so lemons lay on the scrubbed pine sideboard. Silver serving pieces were everywhere. A pink and white box of sugar cubes sat next to plates of cookies and wafers. Nana commanded a counter covered with knives whose blades were so bright she could probably scry in them. Her face was flushed and her hair lifted on the breeze from a ceiling fan. She grinned as we came in.

"What a lovely thing to see you walking through my door again, Gwennie." Nana kissed my cheek. "We have lots to do in the next half hour, but it's fun."

Thelma grunted.

"Oh hush, it is too," Nana said. "Gwen's young and eager to learn, unlike some I could name. Now, Gwennie, wash your hands, please."

I shared the sink space with Thelma. Taking my cue from her, I rubbed liquid soap up to my elbows and scrubbed, as Nana launched into a description of the Sea Horse Inn's guests.

"We have six for tea. The two girls from yesterday—Korean college students on a road trip—" Nana said in an aside to me. "Mr. And Mrs. Heller, the couple from—"

Thelma said something like "the swingers"—could that be right?—over her shoulder to Nana.

"Just her, I think," Nana said, and when I glanced back, I saw her flash Thelma a quelling look. "He seems quite nice. And our new arrivals are three retired teachers driving up to Ashland for the Shakespeare festival."

Thelma grumbled something else. And this time, since I was ready for it, I heard her say, "Took a roundabout route, if you ask me."

"And aren't we glad they did?" Nana murmured, and I was beginning to think I could learn plenty by eavesdropping when Nana began lecturing.

"Now, Gwennie, to prepare a proper tea, check your table first. Be certain you have your caddy spoons, mote spoons, serving plates, sugar tongs, cream pitcher . . ."

"Okay," I said automatically, but Nana saw my confusion and started me off with something simpler.

"Cover that platter with a linen napkin. Yes, the cut glass—very good. We're having a lemon-cream tea today, so select twenty napkins that fit our color scheme. From that drawer. No, *that* one."

While I counted out linen napkins, Thelma began muttering again.

"He's no business leaving her alone at the cottage

with that lot from town causing havoc."

That brought my head up from counting. Without meaning to, I looked to Nana, hoping she'd contradict or clear up what Thelma had said.

Instead, she picked up two lemons with each hand and thrust them my way. Once I'd corralled the roly-poly fruit, she gave me a cutting board and wide-blade knife.

"Lemon slices, not wedges, Gwennie," Nana instructed. "And fan them around the edge of that plate. Then fill the center with lemon bars—those cookies with the powdered sugar topping. Yes, those—but don't forget the doilies underneath."

I had to think fast to catch all that, and when she thought I was engrossed, Nana answered Thelma—in a sharp whisper. "They're harmless, and you can't blame them for venting their high spirits—what with no fishing to tire them out."

Who were *they*? The "lot" from town?

As if she'd caught my mind wandering, Nana jumped back into lecture mode.

"Tea water must go cold into the kettle," Nana said as water rushed from the tap. "It has more oxygen that way," she explained, but you could tell she had a thing or two more to say to Thelma.

I arranged the doily with pretend concentration.

"You're too polite to see them as the riffraff they are," Thelma mumbled, but she wasn't fooled by my focus on the lemon bars, because she cleared her throat, going on louder than before. "Heat the water to 185 degrees, and always measure the tea leaves." She handed me a tin full of aromatic black tea. "Too few and it tastes like water. Too many and it's bitter as rue."

"I don't know how rue tastes, but that's too complicated for me," I said. "I don't want to mess it up."

"A few more lemons then," Thelma said. "Here. A dull knife is more dangerous than a sharp one. Use this."

"Don't be silly," Nana continued. "They're not riffraff."

Pretty quickly I realized she wasn't talking about the knife, and I looked to see Nana recognize she'd said that last part openly.

She sighed and let me in on the clandestine conversation. "You remember Zack McCracken, don't you?"

The name spun in my memory, stirring up embarrassment and anger. Did I recall a blond boy throwing rocks at gulls until they rose in whirling clouds? And sea lions. He'd threatened the sea lions that summered in Mirage Point's sheltered cove.

"Sort of," I said.

"Zack and his family have fallen on hard times, is all," she said quietly, then flicked her fingers as if scattering mosquitoes. "They blame the sea lions for poor fishing, but these things come in cycles. This one's lasted long enough that some of the boys from fishing families have started—"

"Running in packs," Thelma supplied.

As she and Nana bickered, black and red splashed over my memories, and I winced. Had that ever happened to me before? Didn't memories come in images, not colors?

Gradually, I remembered my third-grade crush on Zack McCracken. He'd liked me back, but for proof of it, he'd trailed me down to the cove and shot an arrow at one of the sea lions.

Sick, I thought now. Why hadn't he just chased me at recess or written me a love letter on notebook paper like a normal little boy? He should have known the act that was meant to impress me would backfire. I'd pounded him with my fists and chased him up the cove trail, all the way to the street, even though the arrow was a toy and the sea lion's wound little more than a scratch.

Kids who hurt animals grew up to hurt people, I'd heard.

Zack McCracken, I thought, trying to refocus on Thelma and Nana. I hope he'd forgotten he ever knew me.

"They do pal around in a group," Nana admitted, tempering Thelma's description. "And they've been known to make remarks some folks find unnerving. A few of them break rules—"

"And laws!" Thelma insisted.

Nana leaned forward, arms crossed on the counter. She was probably more tired out by this talk than by her broken leg.

"Gwen," Nana said, touching my hand. "We've had no trouble at Mirage Beach, but they've marked up some Siena Bay shops with graffiti. Still, no matter what folks say, I don't believe they were involved in harming that hitchhiker."

I was not feeling good about living alone.

"Trounced him, they did, and broke his nose." Thelma removed her soiled apron then took a clean one from a cupboard.

"The sheriff is fairly certain the homeless man had a quarrel with companions, and they caught a ride out of town, leaving him behind."

"'Fairly certain,' my rosy red bum."

"Thelma!" Nana gasped.

Thelma didn't act contrite. She tied her apron strings so vehemently that her wrists cracked.

Then, with the bow at the back of her waist looking like a white butterfly, Thelma started for the parlor, gesturing for me to follow. "Now, to *serve* a proper tea . . ."

The sooner we started, the sooner I'd finish. I lifted my tray and hurried after Thelma.

I wanted to be inside my cottage with the doors locked, before dark.

❖ ❖ ❖

How could I not stay for dinner? All through teatime, I'd hardly noticed the guests because I'd been concentrating on serving correctly. But I had noticed the food, and it looked great.

While Nana and Thelma had soup and sandwiches for dinner, I feasted on poppy-seed scones with lemon curd, delicate shortbread wafers, and cup after cup of Ceylon tea.

"I daresay, you're a little weary after your drive and your first day of work," Nana said, "but tomorrow we'll go into Siena Bay, if you like."

"I wouldn't mind being a hermit for a few days," I said, yawning as if it was weariness keeping me here at Mirage Beach.

Nana didn't say a word about facing those who remembered my childhood scandal. Still, when she reached into her skirt pocket and pulled out her scrying mirror, I wasn't a bit surprised.

Thelma drifted toward the sink with the cleared dishes, but Nana gestured me to stay seated at the kitchen table. Nana rarely used polish on her copper mirror. Sometimes she made a paste of lemon juice and salt to burnish it. More often, though, she cut a fresh square of cheesecloth, folded it just so, and rubbed. That's what she did now.

I lifted my teacup and pressed it against my lip, waiting. Most people like to read their horoscopes in the newspaper, and there was an element of that kind of fun in scrying. But it was more personal.

I only remembered Nana telling good fortunes. But is that all she saw?

She took a deep breath, settled further into her chair, and stared at the copper mirror. Her forehead and the corners of her mouth were suddenly free of wrinkles. Her eyes were wide open, but focused far beyond the mirror.

Water swished quietly over the dishes. From the living room came the sound of the grandfather clock's pendulum, swinging.

Nana lifted her hand and made a brushing movement. Was she banishing a cloud that hovered between her and the message in the mirror?

Outside, the waves rushed, broke, and sighed.

"Rerun!" Nana snapped, and struck the tabletop with both palms.

"Pardon me?" Thelma turned from the sink, hands dripping soapsuds. She looked as surprised by the word as I felt.

Dread settled at the nape of my neck as Nana scooped up the mirror, deposited it back into its pouch, and pulled the drawstrings tight.

"Though I can't fathom why," Nana told me, shaking

her head. "I'm getting some old tale—a s-story instead of your reading."

She made a *what's up with you?* gesture toward the mirror as if it could see. After that she rubbed the space between her brows, then touched her fingertips to her right temple.

Thelma pounced on the gesture.

"You're exhausted, is what. Far be it from me to tell another adult what she should do," Thelma began. Then, of course, she did just that. "Gwennie's here to help, so let her, while you sit in the parlor, reciting those old tales—which sound like they're fair strugglin' to be told—to your guests."

Nana made a dismissive gesture, but Thelma pressed on.

"That's what makes the Sea Horse Inn special," Thelma scolded. "What brings folks back again and again is your special brand of hospitality. Any fool can take care of kitchen chores."

Though that wasn't exactly the way I would have put it, Thelma was right.

I squatted next to Nana's chair and made her look at me, face-to-face.

"Nana, I'll feel awful if you don't let me help."

The distressed look left her face. She hugged my shoulders.

"Since you two are determined to browbeat me"—

Nana yawned and her gauzy sleeves fell back as she stretched her arms toward the rafters—"we'll try again when my mirror's in a better mood, silly thing." She stood, slipped the mirror into her skirt pocket, and kept her hand covering it while her blue eyes met mine. "Because Gwennie, I would cut out my tongue before telling that fortune to you."

Chapter Three

❖

The beach was still purple with twilight when I reached Cook's Cottage.

When I set my foot on the porch and inched open the screen door, I heard a rustling overhead, which told me the bird had returned to her nest. I barely breathed as I slipped my key into the lock. It opened the door on the first try.

"Gumbo girl!" I called as I stepped inside and locked the door behind me.

I put a brimming fruit basket and a covered plate of cheesecake on the table. No one left Nana's kitchen empty-handed.

Next I scooped my sleepy cat from the couch.

Gumbo's face was half orange and half white. A vee

of black covered her forehead. Blinking, she gave my cheek a lick.

"It wasn't so bad," I told her. "Except for the part where I had to stand and ask, 'Would you like milk, lemon, or sugar? One lump or two?' about a hundred times. And the part where I have to be back over there by seven in the morning."

I paused to take a breath. If I were home, Mom would have been reading nurses' journals. Dad would have been tapping at computer keys or watching some TV program on forensic blood spatters.

But the cottage sat silent around me.

When Gumbo jumped from my arms and pranced toward the kitchen, I heard each of her steps and the hum of the refrigerator.

I turned on the kitchen light. It gave a buzz like far-away bees. A breeze butted against the wall facing the driveway, and I looked up.

Something moved, and I jumped away from—myself.

I caught my breath, embarrassed that I'd been scared half to death by my own reflection in the window over the kitchen sink.

"You are too dumb," I stuck my tongue out at my reflection and turned off the light.

I tried to work up some enthusiasm for the cheesecake, but couldn't, so I found a place for it in the refrigerator.

Restless, I went upstairs, flopped on my parents' bed,

and tried to read a magazine. The diet and makeup tips didn't hold my attention.

"Okay." Exasperated, I addressed the window looking out to sea. All day I'd shoved the memories away. If I let them have their way for just a few minutes, maybe this fidgety feeling would stop. "Take over."

Nothing happened, of course, because I remembered so little about that night. What I did recall was filtered through the mind of a little kid.

I knew I'd been on Little Beach, not Mirage Point.

I knew Thelma had lied about that, but why?

I knew I'd talked with someone. He hadn't been a hallucination, but he probably wasn't a Gypsy, either.

I knew he hadn't hurt me.

Who *did* know the truth? Not Mom and Dad, though I hadn't exactly grilled them for details. That night meshed with the fear and embarrassment I felt over sleepwalking. By the time I wanted to talk about it, it just seemed too late.

Thelma knew something, and so, probably, did Nana. The sheriff had moved to Boston. I knew that from Dad. But really, none of them knew anything because there'd only been the two of us on that beach.

Everything else was supposition and gossip.

During one of my talks with Dr. Cates, he'd asked if the boy on the beach was a selkie. Of course I'd heard the local legends of magical creatures that transformed from sea lions to humans. Now I realized he was guessing the stories had gotten mixed into my sleepwalking dream. But then I'd given the idea serious consideration.

My Gypsy boy had been darkly handsome, and he'd certainly had a way with the waves, but I hadn't seen him shrug off a sea lion's skin or gesture with webbed hands. He didn't have little flat-to-the-head sea lion ears, either.

No, I told Dr. Cates, I'd seen all of him there was to see. He'd looked quite human.

I took an elective class called Myths and Monsters during my freshman year at Valencia High. I didn't try to fool myself. I knew I was still looking for answers. When we had to do a term project on a myth or monster, I chose selkies, and the thing I discovered is that selkie stories are almost prehistoric, pre-Christianity for sure, and details vary.

Legends only agree upon three things. Selkies are friendly, heroic, and so handsome they take your breath away.

Lots of stories mentioned the number seven, and though they never recounted that rhyme, I'd never forgotten it.

"Beckon the sea, I'll come to thee," I whispered to the room. "Shed seven tears, perchance seven years."

I'll come to thee. The language was old-fashioned. It sounded formal, too, although my sophomore English teacher had told us that Shakespeare and people who'd lived in those days would've used *you* to talk with someone formally. *Thee* was reserved for friends.

Whatever.

I hadn't called him back. I never would.

Still, reciting those words into the silence had given me nonstop chills.

The sure cure for silence was television, even if it was a miniscule black-and-white set from my parents' college days. I ran downstairs with Gumbo at my heels and plopped onto the brick-colored couch.

TV did the trick.

I was two hours into a *Brady Bunchathon* and a bag of nacho chips when Gumbo jumped on the sill of the big living room window.

The couch was on the same wall as the door, facing the shelf that held the TV, and the window was on my left. If I concentrated on the screen, I could ignore those sheer curtains.

Gumbo didn't find it quite so easy. Switching her tail, she stared out into the night. If I hadn't already been startled by my own reflection, the sight of her golden eyes, mirrored by black glass, would have freaked me out.

"Knock it off, kitty," I said forcefully. Of course she didn't.

In fact, she vibrated with a rumble which rapidly turned into a growl. This wasn't the hunting hum she reserved for birds. Gumbo sounded almost vicious.

I couldn't help looking, but I didn't get up and go to the window.

Suddenly she darted at the glass as if she wanted to leap through. She banged her nose hard enough that she fell, twisting to get her feet beneath her.

This had gone beyond creepy, but there was no way I'd go outside. Not to investigate. Not to run for help.

I couldn't call the Inn, because I had no phone. Even if I had one, I wouldn't want Nana or Thelma running down here for a false alarm. Not that Nana could run these days.

After awhile, sinking into the couch, I convinced myself Gumbo had only seen another cat. She was quite the flirt, my Gumbo. She sounded fierce, but she liked yowling in the moonlight, twining around tomcats, driving them crazy. Maybe she was just playing hard to get.

My eyelids were drooping when I heard her hiss.

"You're spayed," I told her gently. "Get used to it."

But then I remembered the footprint. And "that lot" from the village. And Zack McCracken.

I sat up straight and released the breath I was holding, when I saw Gumbo had turned her attention to cleaning a paw, with her back to the window. I forced myself to turn back to the Bradys, and a few minutes later Gumbo was curled on my lap.

"Boy, that Marsha makes me glad I'm an only child," I told her.

Pushing off my thighs for a single leap, Gumbo returned to the sill.

Even though I knew the deck around the cottage creaked, and I'd hear anyone who came near the house, I thought of the shoulder-high blackberry bushes. They'd make a great hiding place. Feeling brave, I left my safe couch and crossed the room. I felt vulnerable and exposed as I removed Gumbo from the windowsill.

"Bedtime for you!" I said, and when she tried to squirm free, underlining her request with claws, I held her at arm's length and carried her upstairs.

I should have tidied downstairs, but my hands were shaking. I wasn't going back down there until dawn.

At least I'd be in bed, under the kissing-fish quilt, if someone broke in. Vain as it sounds, if there *was* an ax-murderer out there, I did not want my body discovered amid a bright orange litter of nacho chips.

I made it through the night.

Gumbo survived her crisis of nerves and passed out on my chest. I could feel her weight as I surfaced from sleep.

Opening my eyes in the loft was like waking up inside a rainbow. I rolled from beneath Gumbo, pulled myself upright, and just stared.

The loft window showed silvery ocean all the way to

the horizon. An iridescent sky glimmered pink, green, and blue like the inside of an abalone shell.

Last night I'd set the bedside clock radio for six fifteen, though I didn't have to be at the Inn until seven, to help with seven thirty breakfast. It was 5 A.M.

I couldn't believe it. The last time I'd been up this early, I'd been waiting for Santa Claus. There was no time difference between Valencia and Mirage Beach, or that would have explained it.

A gray and white gull skimmed right by the window, turning its head to study me. I gave a wave, amazed at how quickly my life had rolled back in time. As a kid, I'd begged to take my nap upstairs.

The only thing missing was the sound of the ocean. When I was little, I could hear gulls calling and the *shushing* of the ocean.

Then I remembered the skylight.

I reached under the bed, found the hooked pole right where it was supposed to be, and wound the window open until the morning air brought the sea sounds inside.

Waves broke, then sighed as if they were searching, not finding, then coming back, never giving up the search, returning again and again.

Gumbo jumped to the floor, stretched, and inflicted a cursory clawing on my parents' old Persian rug.

"Mrow?" she asked, inquiring after breakfast.

"Downstairs, remember?"

Waving her tail, she waited for me to lead the way. When I did, her paws touched my heels at every other step. Once we reached the kitchen, she crunched and gorged as if she hadn't acted like a possessed animal just last night.

Morning's great that way. You can cry yourself to sleep and wake up wondering what the fuss was over.

Since my suitcases were still in my old room, I dressed there in a sleeveless white shirt and a navy blue pull-on skirt.

I couldn't wait to go outside. If Mom were here, she'd tell me to eat breakfast. But I was in charge of myself, so I grabbed an apple from the fruit basket and opened the door carefully.

As I did, a swallow burst from the mud nest. A dart of blue-gray and ivory, she sailed over my head, then soared with pointed wings.

Was she out to catch breakfast for herself or were there babies inside? I'd have to make sure Gumbo stayed locked up. A featherless, fallen hatchling would be just her style.

That's my kitty. It didn't matter that she was sleek and well fed. Show her quick-moving prey and, assuming it's smaller than she is and helpless, she was all over it.

I shut the door firmly behind me, then surveyed my domain.

Three paths led away from the cottage.

One went left to the driveway. Standing a couple steps out from my deck, I could see my yellow Bug was still there. Whatever Gumbo had heard last night, it hadn't been car thieves.

From the driveway, I could turn left and go up to the highway or turn right and go over the dunes, through the sea grass to Little Beach. From there, I could turn south, and, if I were in good shape—I am, but not as good as when I was diving—I could jog to Siena Bay.

I hadn't been to Siena Bay in years. According to Nana, it had changed from a fishing village to a tourist town. While that was sort of a shame, I bet it meant I could get a whipped cream–topped mocha at an espresso bar. I weighed that against the possibility I'd be late for my first day of work, and considered the second path.

That trail ran hard north, straight to the Inn. By Dad's calculations, I'd reach the Inn in two minutes, and though I've never had a real job besides babysitting, it's my opinion that anyone who'd show up an hour early for work is trying too hard.

The middle path began as part of the Inn path, then veered left to Mirage Point.

That's the path I took. As I walked, tossing the apple like a juggler, I looked ahead and my steps slowed.

Mirage Point was a finger of earth that pointed toward the Orient.

A sturdy wooden fence marked the end of the path,

to keep Inn guests from tumbling down to a watery death. There's a rounded apron of dirt just beyond that fence, where you could watch the waves rock over the black boulders below.

But it's not all boulders and jagged rocks. If you stood there long enough, concentrating, you'd see a misty green circle of open water, surrounded by petals of white foam. It would take guts and a kind of faith I didn't have to do it, but if you dove *right there*, you'd be safe.

I dashed a hand over my forehead, surprised I'd remembered that spot so clearly. But I'd always wanted to dive from Mirage Point. Anyone could see it was the ultimate diving challenge. It would be exactly like flying.

As a child, I'd talked all the time about trying it. Of course, my parents vetoed the idea. Repeatedly.

Looking at it now, I could see why they had. The Point is as high as two two-story houses piled one on top of the other.

When we moved to Valencia, my parents used my desire to leap as an incentive to give me diving lessons. They never actually said that if I got good enough, they'd let me plunge off Mirage Point, but I thought it was understood that's what I was building up to.

One night I found out they had other motives.

I'd been upstairs doing homework and had come down to sharpen a pencil. I overheard them talking in the kitchen. Mom was making pastry, and Dad was stirring nutmeg into pumpkin pie filling, so it must have been November.

"It's perverse," Mom was saying, "the way I keep asking myself what would have been worse—if she'd jumped off the Point, head first into the darkness, or been alone longer with that man. Neither of them happened," she said, sounding as if her throat was raw and sore. "Why do I keep wondering?"

"It's human nature," Dad comforted her. "Parents rehearse their nightmares so that if the worst happens, they can go on."

Mom gave a grim laugh. "Our paranoia keeps them alive, I guess."

There'd been an avalanche of cookie sheets from a cabinet then, so I didn't hear every word, but it turned out Mom and Dad hoped diving would tire me out. They wanted me to sleep deeply and dreamlessly.

They also hoped I'd grow into the kind of scholar-athlete who earned scholarships, and for a while it looked like that might work out.

I had a knack for diving.

After those first lessons, my teacher asked me to be on the rec-center diving team. Next I made the school team. By the time I was a sophomore, I was the second-ranked diver in my region. And that's when I quit.

I convinced my parents I'd just lost interest, so it

didn't occur to them to caution me not to dive off the Point this summer.

Now that I was here, without them to yell "no," did I want to try it?

Suddenly it was as tempting as shedding those seven tears to see if that Gypsy boy would return. If I wanted to take that dive or squeeze out those tears, no one could stop me.

I walked down to the Point. With each step, the sound of waves on rocks grew louder.

Three-quarters of the way there, yards short of the fence, I changed my mind.

A faint trail showed in the weeds. It was no wider than a rabbit's body, and it led down to the cove. Once the trail started down, the sea grass vanished, leaving bare rocks slick with sea spray.

That's the path I took.

Ever since I'd climbed out of the VW yesterday and started up Nana's porch, I'd wanted to go to the cove. When I saw the wet footprint on my porch, I wanted to go to the cove. When I breathed the salt air this morning, I wanted to go. No big deal, except it wasn't an ordinary "want."

It was as if I were falling. A rare gravity pulled me to the cove.

I heard the gentle morning *arfs* of mother sea lions caring for their pups.

The trail twisted like a spiral staircase. With each step the sounds became clearer, but a stone arch blocked my view. I saw the cove in my memory, though: a tiny beach studded with rocks next to a grotto full of swaying green light.

Before, I hadn't been allowed to go there for fear the tide would come in and trap me.

The cove's sand was pink with dawn, and it was hard to tell the difference between sea lions and rocks.

Their "arfs" grew louder, but they weren't really afraid. Glistening silver, black, and dark mink brown, the mothers edged their pups away from me.

Trying to be inconspicuous, I sat on a boulder facing them, with my back to the grotto.

I loved watching the sea lions move. They're not like seals, which drag themselves along by front flippers. Sea lions really walk like lions. Actually more like dogs. They get up and use all four of their flippers.

There were about a dozen mothers with babies. The cove was shallow and warm. Pups paddled around, learning to swim. They were so cute you wanted to hug them, to nuzzle your face into their plush fur, but you'd be taking a real chance.

Sea lions are a protected species, and they rarely hurt anything unequipped with gills. Walk too close, and they'll launch into the cove and swim away. Usually.

The bulls were exceptions.

For as long as I can remember, Nana has called every big male sea lion who's protected the cove "Bull." This summer's Bull must be out for a swim, but I stayed alert. Those big males weighed hundreds of pounds and flashed terrifying teeth.

Nana has a gruesome picture of a guest who tried to pet one. She makes people who express an interest in visiting the cove look at it. After that, most stay away.

Behind me I heard footsteps in the water.

Slowly I turned my gaze from the sea lions, and I saw him. Sun glistening on water can make you see things that aren't there. But he was only a few yards away.

He sat on a flat rock just outside the grotto.

My gaze swept the cove, trying to make sense of the fact that he hadn't been there just a minute ago. Okay, so I'd been sort of hypnotized by the beach, but why hadn't the sea lions reacted to his approach?

Maybe he speaks their language, I teased myself. After all, in those old legends, selkies ruled as princes among the sea lions.

He was handsome enough to be a selkie. That's for sure.

His cut-off jeans were drenched. He had the blackest hair I'd ever seen. His bare feet reminded me of sculpture, and the corners of his eyes tilted. He wasn't Asian,

I didn't think, but he could be Italian or Greek. His nose might have been broken once.

The details quit coming when he moved.

He leaned back on arms braced behind him. He wore a lazy smile, and he was totally immersed in sunning himself. It was a good thing his eyes were closed, because I couldn't stop staring.

His sun tan was gold and so smooth, he might have been wearing fresh skin. I wanted to skim my fingers along that dip where his neck turned into shoulder.

What? Why was I thinking about touching a stranger?

I tucked my fingers into my palms and locked my fists with my thumbs.

"You never called," he said, and then he opened his eyes.

I drew a deep breath. In my mind, bells clanged like they do when the merry-go-round stops and you have to dismount from a purple horse. Fantasy over.

"That would be because we've never met," I told him.

He looked astonished. "You don't remember?"

"I'd remember, believe me," I said.

"It was here," he said, trying to give my memory a nudge as he studied me with serious brown eyes.

"Here?" I asked. Although he had that peculiar Celtic rhythm to his speech, like the old folks along this beach, I really didn't think he was a local guy.

His description of "here" came with a vague gesture that took in the entire California coast. When he moved that way, sinews flexed from his forearm to his index finger.

I was doing it again, and I do *not* ogle strangers.

"When?" I asked, I guess because I wanted it to be true.

He looked down at the sand between his feet. This was not a hard question. He was either dumb or a really bad liar. I was beginning to work up some real irritation with myself and him when water dripped from his hair to his chest.

I tried to draw a breath, but it got stuck.

That dark gold tan flowed over his muscles and under the droplet. He must work out, because he had a really nice chest. In fact, he had really nice everything.

He looked up as if he'd finally formulated an answer.

I was so embarrassed he'd caught me staring, I got mad.

"You had me going there for a minute," I snapped.

"Going where?" he asked, but the question didn't sound sarcastic.

All the sea lions had fallen silent, and I heard how sharply I'd spoken. He looked confused, so I softened what I'd said.

"It's not a very original pick-up line. That's all," I told him. What if he wasn't a native speaker of English? He did have that accent.

My brain was working up more excuses for him when I noticed the way his wet hair clung in little thorn shapes to his cheekbones. Something about that stopped me. I recognized him. Almost.

His face lit with a puppyish joy. He flushed a little.

As if he could read my mind, he said, "I knew you'd remember."

All this time he'd been sitting on that sun-warmed rock, but now he stood. He was taller than I'd expected. At least six feet tall. Muscular. And intimidating. When he moved toward me, I backed up a step.

He noticed. His eyes darted past me, as if he'd block my escape.

Not good, I thought, and a jolt of adrenaline made me hyperalert.

"I've got to go to work," I said.

"Wouldn't you rather stay here?" His head tilted back, and he seemed to take in the blue sky vaulting over the red-brown rock walls. He got that same look he'd worn with his eyes closed, when he was basking, taking joy in the sun's warmth on his wet skin.

"It's my first day of work."

He gave a "so-what?" shrug. Maybe he was rich.

When he reached toward my arm, the adrenaline rush returned. This was going too fast. It didn't matter how cute he was.

"They're counting on me," I said.

He could have reached me, but his arm fell back to his side. He looked resigned and maybe a little disgusted.

As I started back up the trail to Mirage Point, I waved, then I heard him take a breath.

I knew he was going to say something. I kept moving, but I did look over my shoulder.

"Gwennie," he called. "Will you come back this time?"

I took that steep path at a run.

How did he know my name?

CHAPTER FOUR

❖

All day, I wondered if he'd show up at the Sea Horse Inn.

He could be a guest I'd met there when I was a child. Or someone who'd attended Siena Bay Elementary school. It was possible I'd met him at a Northern California swim meet.

But the thing is, I would have remembered. I'm not the boy-crazy, crush-a-week type, but if he'd asked me to call him, I would have melted on the spot.

He looked like a competitive swimmer. My thoughts kept circling back to that fact, but it didn't feel right.

Something embarrassing, which made me glad no one could read my mind, was that I'd never noticed a guy's skin before. I actually thought about it as I set Nana's table with fine silver.

As I washed dishes after the guests had drifted away from breakfast, I replayed his brown eyes, which shifted expression from devoted, to playful, to predatory. Something about him wasn't normal.

I told Nana I'd work for her all day long to help her catch up on things she couldn't do with her injured leg. The truth was, I was afraid to walk back to my cottage.

Where was he? Who was he?

Yes, it was broad daylight, but what if he was waiting for me? What if that had been his footprint on my porch?

I wanted to ask Nana or Thelma if the leader of the Siena Bay pack was pathologically handsome. But I didn't.

Instead, I put my anxiety to good use. I washed windows for Nana and didn't glance up when I did those on the seaward side of the Inn.

My only break was when my parents called, having waited a record twenty-four hours to check on me. I told them Gumbo and I had made it through the night just fine.

Of course I didn't mention Gumbo's hallucination at the window or the guy in the cove, so when I talked to Mom, she admitted they were going away for a week, camping in Colorado. They hung up happy as they could be without having me in sight.

After that, I spent two hours on my knees in the sun, sanding weathered boards on the widow's walk, because Nana swore that the rough footing had caused her to trip. I didn't look toward the Point.

By the time I finished, I was sweaty, dirty, and I'd worked the craziness out of my system. The guy I'd talked with wasn't abnormal; he was foreign.

Next time I saw him, I'd ask where he came from. And that would be that.

It never occurred to me that I wouldn't see him again.

Cooled by lazy overhead fans, the inn was an oasis after my hours outside.

"These jeans will never be the same," I apologized, as I met Nana in the kitchen. I'd borrowed a pair of her old jeans to do chores, and the knees had gone from white to cobwebs.

"Nor you either, by the look of you," Thelma said.

My eyes were still dazed by sun glare, but I noticed my arms were sunburned and my hands blistered. I'd pinned my hair into a knot, but most of it had fallen down.

I was in no condition to serve tea, but it was nearly four o'clock.

"Those jeans were destined for the rag bag anyway," Nana said. "And you've just enough time for a quick bubble bath."

I'd opened my mouth to protest when she said, "I'll draw it for you myself, and I promise you'll find it quite restorative."

Since Nana believed in the power of herbs long before aromatherapy had been invented, I wasn't surprised that the collarbone-deep bath smelled tropical and lush.

Her room was on the sea side of the house, so even in the little tiled bathroom, I could hear the waves.

Limp with relaxation, I still managed to climb out, towel off, and find the dress Nana had laid out for me.

It was one of those dresses that's infinitely adjustable. Kind of counterculture looking, but cool. Made of crinkled ivory cotton, it had random sparkly stuff like confetti on the skirt, and the top left my arms bare. For once the muscles left from my days as a diver didn't make me look manly, just fit.

It nipped in at the waist and swirled around my knees.

My wet hair could have used some work, but there wasn't time. Looking in Nana's mirror, I fluffed it with my fingers. Mom called the color "red amber."

Before it could fall into high-humidity waviness, I pinned it up.

Knowing Nana wouldn't care, I poked around in her makeup. I smoothed on Hushabye Blue eye shadow, a little mascara, and transparent lip gloss, and decided I looked all of seventeen.

That guy—who knew my name even though I didn't know his—had looked older. Maybe nineteen or twenty.

I slipped on the sandals I'd worn this morning, twirled the skirt, and smiled at my mirrored self. Except—I couldn't see her. Sunlight streamed in from the seaside window, creating a dazzle on the mirror which made me squint.

I blinked and turned away, still grinning. Who could blame me for feeling glad there'd be no one waiting up for me tonight and for feeling a little bit wild?

Serving tea turned out to be easier than yesterday, and I actually looked at the guests. There were only five of them today.

As I peered up from my tray of sugar, milk, and lemon slices, I decided the woman whose hair was sprayed into a brass-blond helmet must be the one Thelma was saying snide things about yesterday. Mister and Mrs. Heller, that was it, but I wished I could remember what she'd said about them besides the fact that the husband—the balding guy had to be him—seemed nice enough.

I liked the other guests better, though I'm sure Nana didn't want me prioritizing them. Still, the three English teachers guessed that I was about to be a senior, asked if I liked English, and warmed me with approving smiles when I said literature was my favorite subject.

They sat together on Nana's couch, though it was a tight fit. They were all a little overweight, but not in a bad way. They looked comfortable and happy. The fluffy blonde and the one with short black hair bracketed the one with faded reddish hair and glasses.

They were joking and helping themselves to chocolate éclairs when I realized they could be Mandi and Jill with me in the middle, about forty years from now. Except I couldn't see Mandi going on a road trip which ended at a Shakespeare festival.

"Mrs. Cook's promised to tell us a myth," said the teacher with the black hair. "I hear she knows dozens."

"She does," I said proudly. "She's my grandmother."

"What a fortunate girl," said the bespectacled one.

I agreed and refilled her teacup.

Nana sat in a wing chair in the parlor, playing hostess. Her purple, paisley skirt draped to the floor, covering her walking cast. With her many-ringed fingers and wispy hair, she looked like an elfin queen.

I worked as I listened, refilling teacups and passing trays, always wondering if that boy was nearby.

When Nana settled back in her chair, the parlor grew quiet. Her eyes rested on the Inn's green lawns, which rolled down to the beach, sending back echoes of the waves. She told the tale as if she'd heard it many times and memorized it.

"Long ago on these shores, there lived a fisherman's daughter named Larina. Though she was a sunny, healthy girl, everyone knew she was destined to be a spinster.

"Not that she wasn't kind. She took hot tea to fishermen as they mended nets, huddled against harsh winds. She was friendly, too, tolerating the bellows' hot breath to keep the blacksmith company as he mended her mother's cooking pots. And Larina was patient, for she could be found chatting as best she could with the shopkeeper whose never-ending stammer made villagers eager to escape his company.

"But Larina saw most men as brothers and they, in turn, considered her a sister. Still, she counted herself content—until she learned the way of true happiness.

"One night a dream compelled her to walk down to the darkling shore . . ."

Nana's voice trailed off, and it was weird. Though I was probably the only one in the room who had reason to shiver at this, something in her voice made two of the teachers rub their arms as if chafing away gooseflesh.

"Making her way to the ocean's edge wasn't easy for Larina. Only a crescent moon showed, thin and bright as a slash in the black sky, glowing with the luminous promise of what waited on the other side.

"Against the rearing waves a gentleman appeared. Tall and slim he was, and wet. Although he spoke an unknown language, he gave her to understand he'd been bathing for his own amusement!

"Larina was shocked." Nana peered at us in mock-disapproval, and everyone laughed.

"No man in Siena Bay plunged into the wayward sea unless his vessel overturned. Then he would struggle back aboard or into shore as soon as he could.

"But this gentleman was different." Nana paused. Someone sighed, but it wasn't me. "Though they spoke different languages, each heart greeted the other silently. 'Hello sweet friend,' they seemed to say. 'Why have you waited so long to appear?'"

At this, Mrs. Heller shifted, tossed back the last of her tea, and snapped her fingers in my direction.

The fluffy blond English teacher tsked her tongue disapprovingly, while I poured more tea.

Nana ignored us all.

"More full of wonder than she was fear, Larina slipped out to meet her dark gentleman each night. When she imagined her father having him arrested for his intentions, she feared jail would kill him just as surely as stoning. And yet she couldn't stay away. Just as the waves return to the shore, Larina returned to him, and one night she learned what it was that made him so different.

"She came upon him naked and silvered with moon glow, resting beside a sea lion's skin, and knew him for a selkie, those cousins of fairy folk that transform from sea lion to human as they please.

"'Why didn't you tell me?' She demanded an answer, but he was confused by her outrage. In the way of animals, he knew they were different and knew it did not matter. He also knew, as creatures do, that their time together would last but a season."

Mrs. Heller started to rise, as if the story had ended, but her husband touched her arm. Giving him a frown, she sat back, crossed one leg over the other, and jiggled her foot as Nana went on.

"Out of faith, Larina forgave her dark gentleman, but she did not understand.

"You may ask if they were lovers or merely companions. Was there a handfast ceremony at the ocean's edge?" Nana shrugged. "The legend doesn't say, but one night Larina came to their secret cove despite a terrible storm. Winds tore her hair. Rain ruined her gown. Waves towered red-black above her. Larina waited all alone, trying to forget that selkie's blood, shed by a human hand, causes an awful storm, and only another human hand can heal the wound and end the storm. She waited, and still he did not come.

"Larina changed in that storm. Always the mildest of girls, she screamed a vow into the tempest. She would help, she would heal him if she could! But the merciless stars just winked at her, and by dawn—" Nana broke off. "Well, as a matter of fact, many said she'd gone mad.

"From that night on, Larina lived alone, called an old maid by some, a sea witch by others, until"—Nana smiled and held up one finger like a candle—"one night seven years later, when the moon peered through a slit in the black sky, Larina went again to the shore, and drowned."

The teachers sat back suddenly, like they'd suffered whiplash from Nana's abrupt ending. Except, of course, she wasn't done.

"At least," Nana went on in a wheedling tone, "that's what folks said. Suicide, they decided, because the villagers who went to her cottage found the floors swept, the pantry bare, and the hearth cold. The only thing they could not explain was the wreath of seaweed, braided in lovers' knots, decorated with shells, lying on Larina's narrow spinster's cot."

Nana dipped her head to the soft applause that followed.

"Oh, well done," said the teacher with glasses, patting the hand of the fluffy blonde, who looked as if she might cry.

"Beautiful," said the teacher with the black hair.

"What do you do around here for nightlife?" asked Mrs. Heller.

The flutter of appreciation stopped.

Into the silence, the brassy blonde added, "You know, clubs, dancing, that sort of thing."

Everyone in the parlor was speechless. Talk about breaking a spell.

Nana wore a vague smile, as if she were still coming out of a trance, and I tried not to be mad, but really, who would stay at the Sea Horse Inn, two hours in each direction from major cities, if she were looking for nightlife?

Her husband was clearly embarrassed.

"I want to walk on the beach and read," he said, rubbing a hand over his balding head. "She wants to boogie."

Mrs. Heller jiggled her china teacup, then set it down with a rattle. Feeling protective of Nana's china, I made a grab for it.

"I'll keep that, hon," she told me, and the smile, which pleated her mahogany skin, told a cautionary tale.

"Of course," I said, making a mental note to use the sunscreen Mom had made me pack.

By now, Nana had been congratulated by the teachers, who then hustled from the room, leaving an air of disapproval behind.

"For real nightlife, you'll have to stay for our Midsummer celebration next weekend," Nana said. "At Mirage Beach and Siena Bay we've all grown up celebrating the summer solstice."

"Sounds kind of pagan and rowdy," Mr. Heller said.

As he winked at his wife and offered me his empty plate, I realized it was six o'clock. Teatime had long since ended.

"Down in the village, there'll be a parade, games, and sales in all the shops, of course," Nana said.

"And up here?" he asked, sitting forward a little.

"We're more traditional at the Point," Nana explained. "We have a bonfire the night before and tell more stories."

The wife rolled her eyes in boredom as I collected dishes to take to the kitchen. I didn't blame Nana for keeping the best part of Midsummer's Eve secret.

Of course I hadn't been to one since I was a little kid, but Midsummer's Eve was sort of rowdy.

You were required to stay up all night, to build huge, sky-scorching bonfires, and dance yourself silly. After rough competitions, a Summer King and Queen were crowned with flower garlands. As a girl Nana had been Summer Queen three years in a row, and her garland crowns, faded to pale pink and lavender despite some kind of chemical preservative, hung over the fireplace as decorations.

"The solstice," the husband mused, as his wife shifted with impatience. "What is that exactly?"

"The first day of summer and the longest day of the year," Nana said. "After the solstice, every day grows shorter, lengthening the nights as the earth turns toward winter."

That always struck me as unfair. At the very beginning, you shouldn't start worrying about the end.

Laden with dishes, I whisked back into the kitchen. Thelma had already cleaned up everything, so I surrendered the plates without protest before returning to the parlor once more.

"We can't stay that long!" The brassy wife was still bickering with her husband as I came back.

"Maybe next year." Nana's voice smoothed over the shrillness as Mrs. Heller stalked from the parlor. "In the meantime, if you walk into Siena Bay and visit Village Books, you'll find a nice collection on local legends, and they're open until nine."

Mr. Heller looked after his wife.

"Would you believe she was a 4-H kid raising rabbits when I met her? For the first three years of our marriage, all she wanted was a farm." He gave Nana a wistful smile. "Do you suppose she changed, or I just didn't know the real her?"

"That's hard to say," Nana began and then something made me interrupt.

"My mom always says she thought she was marrying a lawyer, but he 'grew up' to be an author. She tells me I better be sure I fall in love with the man, not the lifestyle."

"Well, bravo for your sensible mother," Nana said, and the smile that claimed her face showed me how much she loved us all.

Mr. Heller gave us a salute as he left.

Nana stood and smoothed her purple skirt.

"I didn't fib about Mirage Point's festival, exactly," Nana told me as she closed the pocket doors to the parlor. "Our celebration is for local folks, special because it's—" As Nana searched for the right word, I still heard the waves breaking outside. "—traditional. Not because T-shirts are marked 20 percent off."

We both laughed, and I felt a closeness with Nana that I hadn't felt with anyone for a long time. I couldn't think how to say it, so I just started back toward the kitchen. Nana touched my arm. "Leave those dishes for Thelma. I have a different chore for you. It'll only take me a minute to grab my notebook from upstairs."

Holding a handful of skirt in one hand, gripping the banister with the other, Nana started upstairs. It would take her more than a minute to return, I thought, looking after her. Before finding what she was looking for, Nana would tweak the duvet straight on a bed in an empty guest room, check the potpourri in a shell on a hall table, and chat with anyone she met.

The Inn stood quiet around me.

I had time.

I slid the parlor doors open, slipped inside, and closed them behind me. I crossed the polished wooden floor, the hand-loomed carpet, and stepped through the casement windows. A white cabbage moth trembled in the twilight as I passed through Nana's garden.

I crossed the lawn diagonally. Instead of strolling down to the beach, I turned left, drawn to the path which would take me across the bluff to Mirage Point.

I wasn't hypnotized by the sun shimmering in a hot red disk above the ocean. Even though it reminded me of Nana's scrying mirror, I wasn't feeling dreamy. I knew exactly where I was going and how long I had to get back.

I was going to the Point.

I walked all the way out this time. I held my skirts aside as I'd just seen Nana do, and stepped over the guard fence. The cliff dropped away to the sea, and breakers pounded at its base.

The setting sun turned the waves wine red, except for one spot where the water lay quiet and petals of foam rocked around it. There, it was deep.

I knew I could make that dive.

And then I felt someone watching. My biology teacher said it's a feeling left over from primitive times. Sometimes it's like a vibration across your forehead. Other times it's like a ribbon trailing across the nape of your neck. He said it helped us survive.

This time it felt like hands on my shoulders. I could have sworn someone stood behind me, so close that breath moved my hair and tickled my ear.

"Gwen!" Nana called from the seawall around her garden. Her voice sounded a little concerned, but of course it would, since I'd stepped over the fence.

I really hadn't meant for her to see me and couldn't imagine how she had made it upstairs and down so quickly, until I blinked at the horizon. The setting sun was gone.

"Get a grip," I told myself, then shook my head and hurried back.

❖ ❖ ❖

Nana didn't scold me or demand an explanation. She just motioned me back into the parlor and walked toward the front of the house.

"This is a job you're truly suited for," she said, handing me something that looked like a cross between a notebook and a photo album. "It's my garden journal. A seaside garden isn't the easiest sort to keep. In summer it's either baked by the sun or shrouded with salty fog. In winter it's ripped by gales and lashed with sea spray."

When Nana paused, I realized I'd never given her garden much thought. It was just a place you passed through on your way to the beach. And yet, while I was sanding the widow's walk, I'd noticed the Korean students paying it one last visit before they loaded their gear to go.

"Guests often wander the paths," Nana said, "and they want to know what they're looking at. I've always meant to type up some interpretive signs—a short history and romance of the seaside garden, if you will. Still, I've never gotten around to it. So when your mother told me yours was the hand that calligraphed her holiday cards this year, I began thinking you were the one for the job."

Nana opened the notebook to give me a glimpse of faded lined paper that was written on in what appeared to be Nana's handwriting. There was also a brand new pack of cards made of really nice paper, like wedding invitations, only they looked sort of like they had a frame, with a place to write inside.

"This is the kind of job I could really get into," I told her. I'd totally shaken off that dreamy feeling. I couldn't believe I was getting excited about gardening, but the plants had great names. Saltspray rose, white swan, bridesmaid daisies. "Did you draw these, Nana?"

Sketched in pink, green, and apricot pastels, they'd smeared from being slammed in the notebook. Nana dismissed them with a wave of her hand.

"They're nothing. The notes are what matter. No rush about it," Nana said. "Just start with the ones that are in bloom now or will be by the time you leave. I've marked every one with a date."

Nana flipped the notebook closed and presented it to me like a gift.

Behind us a gust of wind sighed through the house, lifting curtains, bringing the smell of fog that was hanging off the coast, waiting for nightfall.

Nana started to turn, then didn't, as if she wanted to forget the sight of me standing on the other side of the guard fence. If she wasn't going to bring it up, neither was I, but I knew I was to blame for her worried expression.

She was trying to treat me like an adult, and I was blowing it.

"I should walk back to the cottage and get started on this," I said.

"Gwendolyn Anne, you'll do no such thing," Nana said. I realized we were standing next to the ornate coat tree near the front door, and Nana was draping her shoulders with a crocheted shawl. "I'm famished, and you look absolutely lovely in that little dress. There's a little farmers' market in town on Thursday nights. I'm going to treat us both to some street food and show you off."

Fear came raging back like the wave that had knocked me off my feet that night years ago. Echoes of old gossip screeched in my memory. In Siena Bay there'd be people who remembered.

"Nana, I really don't feel like it." I tried to look pitiful and overworked.

"Rubbish," Nana said. She tossed me a square of silver-and-black silk, another shawl, I guessed. I caught it. "Bring that, and we won't even have to stop at the cottage."

She hustled me to the door, hands fluttering as if she were shooing gulls away from a picnic lunch.

I opened the front door and stopped before crossing the threshold. Nana's car had been moved around to the front of the Inn. It was a block-long white Cadillac.

"Totally foolish in terms of gas consumption," Nana said, fondly. "But it's a classic, a relic of my midlife crisis, and I plan to be buried in it."

"Nana," I yelped. I didn't know which outrage to address first: her midlife crisis or her funeral plans, so I did neither. "Can you even drive with that cast?" I asked as she took a brass ring of keys from a hook by the door.

"No," she said. "But you can." Then she tossed the keys at me and said, "Catch!"

CHAPTER FIVE

❖

"I think I can walk to the curb from here," Nana joked. She opened her car door and peered down. I was about a foot too far out in the street.

Parking this big boat of a car in a town crowded with tourists and partyers was almost impossible. Siena Bay's main street was blocked off with sawhorses draped with sparkly lights, so I cruised down side streets until I spotted the last parking space on a steep hill overlooking the bay.

Somehow, I maneuvered us into it, but I didn't do a very good job.

"I can make another pass through town," I offered, reluctantly.

"No need, dear," Nana said, releasing her seat belt and climbing out. "They start shutting down at midnight."

Ha ha. It was only seven thirty.

"But do set the parking brake, please."

I set it as hard as I could, then curbed the wheels like I did when I parked on the hills of San Francisco. If Nana's car started rolling from here, it wouldn't stop until it was headlight-deep in sea bottom.

Nana leaned on my arm a little as we walked uphill toward the gathering, which sounded a lot more like a street fair than a farmers' market.

We passed booths with avocados and artichokes; pyramids of kiwi; baskets of blackberries, strawberries, and cherries; but we also saw vendors selling blown glass figurines, hand-carved wooden toys, and pottery mugs in smooth, bulbous shapes.

Music pulsed through the aimless crowd.

"Hear the flute and bagpipe?" Nana asked. "That will be Red and Ian. You remember Red O'Malley, don't you?"

I didn't, but the same stiff breeze off the bay that brought the aroma of exotic food brought the sounds of a Scottish pipe band and the thudding of a drum which echoed my heartbeat.

"The food booths are down this way," Nana said. I let her tug me along, but I was scanning the crowd, looking for a familiar face. One familiar face.

Strings of lights festooned the booths and criss-crossed overhead. Swaying in the wind, they flickered, creating an uncertain twilight.

"Siena Bay has changed a lot, hasn't it?" Nana asked, as if she'd noticed my head swinging around, taking it all in. "The Chamber of Commerce tries to keep the atmosphere of an old fishing village, but—"

I followed Nana's gesture and focused beyond the booths.

I remembered coming down to the docks at dawn with Mom. She'd buy me hot chocolate from Sal's Fish and Chips, which was the only thing open that early. We'd watch sun-browned men shout and sling around nets before putting off into the turquoise water.

Now, though the nautical decorations remained, they draped a dozen places I could find in the Valencia mall.

"Someone must still fish," I insisted.

"They try," Nana allowed. "In fact, most of them still put out to sea every morning, but they have to supplement."

Supplement. Was that a nice word for welfare? Or something shady? Nana had said the gang in town was made up of fishermen's sons with nothing to do.

"They say it's fished out and blame the sea lions and tourists," Nana went on. "I blame it on pollution and the industrial fisheries, but not many listen to an old woman. I'm glad we're up the coast a ways."

Somehow, this little talk didn't dampen our spirits.

Nana bought us savory meat on bamboo skewers and cups of Thai noodles. We drank lemonade, and I kept looking for him.

Nana reintroduced me to old friends of the family. Gina Leoni ran the Siena Bay grocery, Red O'Malley and his brother Ian owned the Buoy's Club bar. Sadie Linnet had been my second-grade teacher before she opened Village Books.

If any of them thought I was crazy before, they must have wondered if I was medicated now. I admit I was distracted. I nodded and smiled and kept scanning the crowd.

It took Red O'Malley's comment to catch my attention.

"Now that you're practically grown, I have a bit of advice for you, Gwendolyn," he said. His gray-red beard and shaggy hair framed eyes that sparkled with a leprechaun's mischief, and I felt an instant warmth toward him. "If you should run into that young man again—"

Mrs. Leoni groaned and threw her hands heavenward. Sadie Linnet tsked her tongue. Nana shook her head, and their reactions told me he was recalling that night seven years ago.

"—you'll want to be checking between his fingers and toes for webbing."

"Like a duck?" I blurted.

"Somewhat like," he said seriously. "But I've known

from the start it wasn't some ordinary boy you saw. He was a selkie."

"I've thought of that," I said politely.

"They're devilish handsome, charmin', and great seducers of women. They don't mean anything by it, mind, it's just their nature, but a girl—"

"Enough, Red," snapped Mrs. Linnet in her teacher's voice.

"Save your stories for Midsummer's Eve," Nana said, "or Gwen might think you're serious."

"Or senile," Sadie Linnet added.

I laughed, but couldn't help noticing that Nana was edging me away from her friends.

"It was nice talking with you all again," I said, and as Nana set out through the throng, I held tight to her. Partly, I was lending her my strong legs, but I didn't want to lose track of her either. When I found the boy from the cove, I wanted to ask her who he was.

"Oh look." Nana gestured with her lemonade cup. "There's Jack Cates. I know you'll want to say 'hi' to him."

That got my attention, big time.

"Nana, *no*."

Whatever questions that man had asked me after "the incident," they had cut to the heart of my fears. You never forgive someone for that. I'm pretty sure the sheriff brought him in to determine my mental state. Was I hiding something? Repressing some trauma? He must have asked about my dreams, too, because I remember blubbering about sleepwalking and people believing Thelma instead of me. I wonder what he ended up telling the sheriff.

Dr. Jack Cates stood at a fruit stand, a living stereotype.

Rumpled psychologist with salt-and-pepper gray beard and glasses, he considered a sample slice of peach as if he were deciding whether he should buy the entire orchard. That analytical attitude chilled me.

He'd invaded my poor little kid brain. Imagine how fascinating he'd find the fact that I hadn't returned to Mirage Beach for seven years, that I'd dropped out of diving just short of making regional champion (my parents had gone off about that so much, even I was beginning to wonder what it *meant*), and, oh yeah, maybe I could tell him about the guy from the cove who communicated his presence telepathically.

On the other hand, he might know more than anyone else what had really happened that night. And I wanted to know.

I tried to pull myself together, gathering energy like I would for a dive, but it didn't work. Instead of feeling powerful, I felt weak and light-headed.

"Nana, I can't talk to him."

"He's seen us now, dear." Nana raised a hand in greeting.

"Well, I'm—" This time when I scanned the crowd, I

looked for an escape. "I'm going to go shop. I'll meet you at the—"

"Ice cream court?" Nana suggested. She nodded toward an area with tables and a blue and white striped awning.

"Right," I said. "In about ten minutes."

"That'll be fine, Gwennie," she said.

I could have kissed her. I should have kissed her. But I bolted instead.

If I'd been with my parents, there's no way I would have escaped.

Turning left, I moved down a side street. I noticed the yuppie stuff giving way to funkier wares. Then I turned right and kept going.

Looking over my shoulder to make sure I was out of Dr. Cates's sight, I realized it was darker on this street. Slowing my strides to a normal walk, I looked up and saw fog coming in, haloing the streetlight.

Here, the booths were less formal, and there were fewer shoppers. Tie-dyed tank tops hung from tent poles pounded into a city-maintained flowerbed. On a rickety card table good-luck bamboo plants had been tortured into weird shapes and stuck in mayonnaise jar "vases."

I spotted what looked like some very cool earrings and headed for them.

"Get outta here, a customer," ordered a girl wearing

more eye makeup tonight than I'd worn in my entire seventeen years.

She wasn't talking to me, but to a group of sleazy-looking guys.

A brass stud pierced her nostril, and spiky hair the color of strawberry soda gave her the look of a scrappy rooster.

"Jade, you promised," one of the guys whined, but she made a motion as if to backhand him, and the guys scattered.

A woman in charge, I thought, smiling. As I got closer I realized she was about my age.

Pinned to a big piece of cardboard, the earrings she had on display were made of beach glass, shells, and twisted wire.

"Hi," I said, bending to look.

She made no response, just lifted her chin as if she were too cool to talk, but maybe she was shy.

I examined a pair of abalone shell ovals, then some loops that looked like hammered silver. Best of all were some dangles with moss green beads that would match a blouse I'd brought to wear while working at Nana's. I was about to ask how much they were when she finally said something.

"That kid has puppies for sale." She pointed at a boy squatting on a blanket beside a weary-looking mother dog and her brood. "Maybe you'll find something you like over there."

"Oh, thanks, but I have a cat who'd—" When I met her eyes, she was smirking.

If that had been a hint that Jade didn't welcome people who window shopped for too long, fine. I straightened up and went on my way.

It was already time to go meet Nana. I walked fast, then glanced back the way I'd come. I was a little turned around, but I didn't ask for help. Jade was watching, smug as if she knew I was lost.

Which I wasn't. I heard Red O'Malley's bagpipes, and I was pretty sure I could take a shortcut to the main street, through an alley that looked like the old Siena Bay.

Nana's silver-and-black shawl had been resting in the bends of my elbows, but now I pulled it up over my shoulders. The heels on my sandals clacked as I entered the alley.

Rotten fish is a smell you don't forget. I clapped my hand over my nose and tried not to breathe. Maybe the low-hanging fog magnified the stench. I hurried toward the music and the dim light at the end of the alley.

The alley narrowed.

I squeaked as a cat battered his way free of a dumpster lid. A skeletal fish, head intact, was clamped in his teeth. A quarreling knot of more cats, three or four at least, erupted from the same dumpster and scattered in yowling pursuit of the lucky one.

"Somebody's catching fish," I muttered, but I

didn't have time to enjoy my own sarcasm.

Dark figures stood between me and the alley's end.

Turn back. My city instincts told me not to worry about how silly and scared I'd look. If I ran, the worst thing that could happen was I'd be laughed at. If I didn't run . . .

But then I took a good look at the three guys. One was too far back to see, but the closest boy was short. I'm five-foot-two, and he looked shorter than me. Plus, his pants were so baggy, he'd lose them in a sprint.

"Looky what we got here," he growled, and suddenly I wasn't scared.

Valencia was a middle-class suburb of San Francisco. It had its share of gang members and thugs. As these boys jostled for a closer look at me, I knew they wouldn't qualify for either group.

Wannabes, I thought. And that was just fine with me.

"Where do you think you're going, little lady?"

"Oh, shut up," I said, and when he stopped in surprise, I strode toward the open space to his right.

I was slipping through, making it, when the second guy grunted. I couldn't help glancing his way. He looked like a young Brad Pitt who'd been living behind one of these dumpsters for a week and decided to crawl out for a joint. He reeked of weed. And though he sure wasn't my type, he was handsome in a doomed way.

I kept walking as he talked. Loud, too, so I'd be sure to hear.

"Guess you been schooled by the little turista, Roscoe."

I was pretty sure that wasn't a Spanish word. And a thug should change his name to something besides Roscoe.

I reminded myself there was still one of them lurking in the shadows. Lounging in that inset doorway? Yes.

That guy was tall, and he wasn't trying to hide. He sort of squared his shoulders.

Of the three, I'd rather face pudgy Roscoe or the moody blond. The one in the shadows was the one to watch.

But I didn't. The smell of corn dogs crowded out the stench of rotten fish, and the sweet trill of a flute was louder than my heels' echo on the slippery concrete.

I was out.

Nana was waiting for me under the blue and white striped awning.

"Your ice cream is melting," she pointed out.

The dish sat across from her on the wooden picnic table. I sat, and even though I wasn't hungry, picked up the plastic spoon and began eating the vanilla ice cream, saving it from becoming part of the pool of chocolate syrup and sprinkles.

"Sorry," I apologized. Boy, I really shoveled that ice cream in, as if my scare demanded I refuel. "I saw some cute earrings, though."

"Did you buy them?"

"No."

"I have a little cash if you'd like to go back," Nana said.

My mixed feelings must have shown. I didn't want those earrings quite enough to return to that dimly lit side street.

"Did something happen?"

"Nothing serious, but I think I ran into some of those bad boys you and Thelma were talking about."

"Those boys?" Nana asked, looking past my shoulder.

My head whipped around to see Roscoe and the shaggy blond strutting down the middle of the street. They didn't push people aside, but their attitude said nothing would make them happier than a scuffle.

"Yeah," I said.

"Zack McCracken, I haven't seen you for so long," Nana called out. "Come over here and say hello."

I sputtered. I didn't spew my ice cream all over the table, but it was touch and go there for a minute. I barely managed to swallow.

My grandmother was a real piece of work. I mean, they weren't actual thugs, but they didn't look like the kind of boys she'd "chat" with.

So this was Zack. He couldn't possibly remember me.

Stoned as he was, he still looked uncomfortable to be singled out. Something in his expression reminded me

I'd met him before third grade, before his bow and arrow attack on the sea lion.

Years ago, Dad had been working on our old station wagon in the gravel driveway, and I'd been bored watching him, when I noticed a kid with a broken down bike up on the road. That was before the traffic increased and it became a serious highway.

"Go ahead and see if he needs help," Dad had said, glancing out from under the hood.

So I did.

Zack and I had been little if it was before third grade. I remember noticing an old bruise on his face. One of his knees had been scuffed up, too, like he'd taken a fall. The only thing wrong with his bike, though, was the chain had slipped off those metal things that make it go around. I knew from experience how to fix it.

By the look of his grease-blackened fingers, he'd been trying to get the chain back on those little metal hooks, but he had a rock in one hand, ready to pound it. I guess ten-year-old boys don't handle frustration well.

I don't know what we said to each other, but I ended up fixing his bike. He'd hated that. In fact, he jerked his bike up off the asphalt, jumped on, and jammed his bare feet against the pedals. He rode off in a rage.

I didn't get it then. By now, I'd noticed guys don't like

to be rescued. Especially by girls. So why had I liked him in third grade?

Zack sauntered up, but stopped in the middle of the street, then joined a few other guys—I didn't see the tall one—to loiter near a store called Merry Mermaid. It was a second-hand clothing store. Maybe they were about to go shopping, but I bet their presence had more to do with the painted wooden statue of a bare-breasted mermaid that guarded the shop's front door.

Instead of saying anything, Zack stopped about four feet from our table and waited.

"Hello Zachary," Nana said.

"Hi," he mumbled. He shot me an appreciative glance before the tough guy scowl locked into place. I guess I looked better under the strings of lights than I had in the alley, but his look wasn't exactly a compliment.

"You're out of school, I see," Nana added.

He made a gesture like "so?" but then he nodded.

"I'm reintroducing Gwendolyn, my granddaughter, to old friends," Nana said.

He looked skeptical, as if he didn't fall into that category. If he remembered me, he didn't care.

"Have a nice vacation," he said, but it sounded more like a curse.

"Oh, she's not vacationing," Nana chuckled. "She's working for me."

Skepticism turned to outright disbelief. "Working?" he asked.

"There's more to do than ever," Nana said. "In fact, there's a summer job for you at the Inn, if you want a little extra cash."

Zack squared off as if he wanted to fight. "I have a job at the arcade. And I'm not homeless, you know."

Talk about defensive, I mean, offering him a summer job wasn't the same thing as—I felt a twinge of guilt—suggesting he lived behind a dumpster.

"Of course not," Nana said, brushing his paranoia aside. "The Marlinspike was still docked in the harbor last time I looked."

The Marlinspike must be a boat. Did that mean he lived on it? The stench from the alley surged up in my memory, and I remembered the heavy clouds of diesel that had hung on the air those mornings I'd gone down to the harbor with Mom. Living on a fishing boat wouldn't be ritzy, that's for sure.

"Hey, yeah," Zack said as he pointed at me. "Gwennie."

He wasn't so wasted he couldn't remember me, I guess.

From everyone else my childhood nickname had sounded sweet. He gave it the singsong whine of a bully, and that's probably why I stood up, walked past the table, and thrust out my hand, forcing him to shake with me.

"So, you livin' in Cook's Cottage?" he glanced over his shoulder at his friends. "Maybe you could use some company."

There was nothing wrong with his words, but the way he said them was scary. A flare of fear made me mean.

"Yeah," I said. "Maybe you could ride your bike over."

He blushed. "Yeah, and maybe I could pay your sea lions a visit."

I didn't recover half as fast as he had. It was a threat. And the way he slung his thumb through a belt loop and raised his chin—that was a dare. *Just tell me to stay away and see what happens.* I could hear it, though he didn't say a word, and I didn't egg him on. I guess Nana didn't hear what I did, because she kind of scolded him.

"The sea lions in Mirage cove are a protected species," Nana said. There was no mistaking her warning.

"We don't need more seal huggers," he growled at me. "Tourists or locals."

I'd heard environmentalists called "tree huggers." I guessed this was the same thing, but it sounded silly.

"Oh now, Zack," Nana tsked. "You know sea lions aren't to blame for this area being fished out."

"No, I don't know that, Mrs. Cook."

Half polite, half rude, he turned and swaggered off down the street. The knot of boys outside the Merry Mermaid broke up and followed after him.

All but one.

SEVEN TEARS INTO THE SEA

It had to be the tall guy who'd been lurking in the alley doorway. The same guy I'd talked to at the cove. I knew that, but I didn't know why my hands were shaking.

"That boy in jeans and the black T-shirt, there by the Merry Mermaid," I said suddenly. "Who is he, Nana?"

For a second I thought she'd miss him. He slipped from the doorway and walked down the street, mingling with the crowd but never disappearing because of his height.

"I don't know," Nana said slowly, but she was rubbing the spot between her brows as she had when she tried to do my reading last night. "Not a local boy, I don't think."

Nana's eyes searched mine.

"I talked with him on the beach yesterday," I admitted.

She drew a deep breath then turned back to watch him.

"He has a certain way about him, doesn't he?" she asked.

So even Nana saw it.

"Kind of," I said. I wasn't really comfortable talking with her about a cute guy. I mean, who would be? To their grandmother?

The street crowd had thinned out when Nana and I started back to the car. It was full dark as I helped her back into the passenger seat, slammed the door, and walked around the back of the car to the driver's side.

Footsteps shuffled along the sidewalk on the opposite side of the street. Headed for the beach, Zack and his crew watched me. I couldn't see them well, but the shortest one, probably Roscoe, noticed me watching.

He was probably smiling as he did it, but I could only see his dark silhouette raise his arm, make a gun of his hand, and shoot straight at me.

CHAPTER SIX

✦

The sea lions woke early, and because I'd left the skylight open all night, so did I.

In minutes I'd swung my feet to the floor, trotted downstairs, and poured myself some juice.

Sitting at the kitchen table in my nightgown, I listened to Gumbo crunch cat food while I paged through Nana's garden notebook. The flower drawings she'd dismissed with a wave of her hand were wonderful.

I flipped to the back of the notebook and found some more drawings folded and jammed in so that the open edges caught in the binding. Once I pulled them free, I had to tip and turn them. Right-side-up and upside-down didn't really apply. They appeared to be random, fairy-tale-looking scenes. Like the garden sketches, they were smeared. Time and friction had blurred them, making it seem as if I were studying them through a rain-streaked window.

Using the card stock and pens from Nana, I began lettering the first entry for her garden guide. Last night, restless with my bellyful of street food, I'd made two resolutions. One, I'd do at least one card each morning. Two, I'd start making good on my summer pact with Mandi and Jill.

"Every day we'll do something new," we'd vowed.

At our all-nighter to end all all-nighters before school started, I wanted to have something to brag about.

The last summer before senior year must be incredible. Adulthood was hovering on the horizon. And then all the fun would end.

It never seemed fair that just when you're old enough to do anything you want, you can't. You have to start working, so there's no time. And if there is time, you're not working, so there's no money.

With great care and too many flourishes, I finished the card. It didn't look bad, I thought, holding it up and blowing on it to dry the black ink.

The last words about having to "take charge lest it run wild," made me grin. No one was in charge of me. Technically, Nana was, but if I stayed up all night listening to CDs or dressed Gumbo in a bikini made of lunch meat and watched her eat it off, no one would ever know.

That last one wasn't the sort of thing I was likely to do, but when the word "bikini" crossed my mind, I knew what I'd do today for my "something new." Before work I'd go for a swim. I had plenty of time to swim, come back up here to change, and make it to the Inn on time. My fingers flew, taming my hair into a single braid, then grabbed a towel and headed out.

Everything before me was draped in fog, which only made this first swim more exciting.

I picked my way down the gravel driveway, headed for Little Beach. If you looked at a map, that wouldn't be its name, but we'd always called it that to distinguish it from the white, sandy beach in front of the Inn.

Walking through the sea grass atop the rolling dunes, I pushed aside fears of what could be hiding in the fog. The bad boys of Siena Bay weren't awake yet, that was for darn sure.

Besides, all I'd have to do to escape anyone was dive into the ocean. I had studied to take the Red Cross life-saving test and passed it. Though I didn't become a life-guard, I'm a strong swimmer. I mean, not being stuck-up or anything, but that's really an understatement.

Aware of the power in my shoulders and legs as I strode along, swinging my arms, I felt good.

When I reached the driftwood-littered beach, I kicked off my flip-flops. Beside them, I dropped the oversize blue jersey I'd used as a cover-up.

Here I didn't cringe with that everyone's-looking-at-the-place-I missed-when-I-shaved-my-legs feeling I got at poolside. Here I was at home. The wet sand cradled my feet, and the fog lay on the water. I breathed the dampness, amazed there was absolutely no boundary between silver-white air and ocean. No wind swirled around me. I might have been standing in a cloud.

The tide was out, and the sea was calm, rolling in to graze my toes with smooth, small waves. *C'mon*, it whispered, *c'mon now.*

I used to know all the sea's voices, and I remembered this one: It was playful and a little impatient.

I wanted to run, splashing through the shallows, and dive in, but another voice—my mom's—kept me from doing it.

Although there hadn't been a shark bite—let alone a full-fledged attack—in these waters since 1976, I rushed through the five points Mom had made me recite each time we went swimming.

One: Is anyone fishing nearby?

It was hard to tell with all the fog, so I listened for the slap of waves on a hull or the racket of a boat engine. I heard nothing but the complaint of a sea bird.

Two: Is it dusk or night?

Nope, as far from those two favorite feeding times as you could get.

Three: Can you see a large number of fish, and if so,

are they flapping around, acting weird?

No. There were some sea lions out there. I could hear them surface and blow through their whiskers, even though I couldn't see them, but they were just mothers from the cove, out cruising for breakfast.

Four: Are you wearing a watch or jewelry or a hair clip that would reflect light and catch the eye of a prowling predator?

Unless the contrast of my winter-pale flesh against my red bikini counted, I was good to go on to the last question.

Five: Do you have any wounds that could possibly bleed?

Not a one. I wasn't a little kid anymore, deliberating over "ow-ies."

So I was safe.

I moved out, letting the waves wet my ankles, knees, thighs. Of course it was cold, but I couldn't resist any longer. I arrowed my hands into the waves and arched my body after them, beginning a shallow dive.

The water was like silk, welcoming my fingertips as I pulled against it, stroking out from shore.

Turning from side to side, my ears caught a deep sound. Big waves threatening, or thunder's rumble? If it was thunder, I was out of here, because after thunder came lightning.

My first diving coach was from Kansas, someplace where they had electrical storms, and he'd always clear the pool at the first rumble of thunder. *Hot as the sun,* was the way he'd described the temperature of a lightning strike. When someone on our team joked about it, wondering what ocean-going fish did during a storm, the coach had snapped, "You have one advantage the fish don't, meathead. You can get out."

I paused, treading water and pushing wet hair from my eyes. Gray translucent waves crested atop each other, but it didn't smell like a storm.

I dove through the base of the next wave and the next, breathing sips of fog from beneath my arm. And suddenly I had company.

A raft of sea lions, sable and sleek, swam just ahead. They didn't welcome me, but they tolerated my presence, which must have seemed clumsy and loud compared to their silent surging.

They'd be heading back to their babies at the cove if there was a storm coming. I'd seen it before, dozens of long, sleek bodies sliding up on the sand. These sea lions weren't worried. The wind swirled a window in the fog, and the seals rose, peering through to see something I couldn't, and then they were off. In their wake a rocking movement pushed me backward.

Let's go! Excitement charged through me, and I followed. Diving, kicking, I pulled my body deeper, following them.

My eyes opened on a watery world of sea lions torpedoing after a school of fish. Better than the Discovery Channel, better than dreams, I saw them career through a kelp forest after silver fish. Flippers fanned past. Hollow stems of kelp bounced against my bare arms. A leathery tail scythed against my leg. Flashing teeth meant for the flickering school of fish reminded me sea lions were at the top of the food chain. I fanned my arms, backing up, removing myself from the sea lions' breakfast buffet.

Time to go back to my world, I thought. Tilting my head back, I sighted the blue-gold surface above. With my destination in sight, I gave what was supposed to be a mighty kick. But I was jerked up short like a dog on a leash. Without a thought for why, I tried again. This time, the yank made me look down.

A leafy amber cord of kelp had snapped taut around my ankle. I squinted. How had it happened? How entangled was I? Why was my leg going numb?

A sea lion rocketed past after the last terrified fish.

My pulse slammed at the side of my neck. My chest swelled with an insane fullness. I needed air. Now.

Glimmers of sun danced above me, reminding me panic and struggle used too much oxygen. I'd need it to swim back up.

Okay, okay, okay. I'm strong. I can break loose.

I bent my knees, gathering my muscle power as if I were launching myself into a dive. Go!

The kelp jerked tight and my head snapped back.

Reserve oxygen.

I could almost remember how many minutes of reserve oxygen a swimmer had. Almost.

Black dots frenzied in front of my eyes. I blinked hard, trying to see past them to the kelp. Should have looked first. Untie it or break it with my hands. But the black-gnat dots crowded out the sight of everything.

It felt good to let my limbs float free.

So this is drowning . . .

I cartwheeled down through green darkness.

I sighed and a chain of bubbles floated past my lips. A golden shaft of sunlight from a sky I might never see again slanted through the water.

A black sea lion darted through the brightness, made a quick curve around me and struck between my shoulder blades. The impact thrust me toward the surface, and the kelp snapped.

My arms and legs took over, striking toward the light. I rose effortlessly in the wake of the black sea lion, until my head broke through.

The first breath made me cough. Seawater had seared my throat. I remembered this feeling and struck off toward the beach.

I might have imagined the fog.

It was gone. Sky and sea spread sparkling turquoise around me.

My limbs felt weak and wobbly. The sea lion, who deserved a Flipper medal for sure, was nowhere in sight. Or maybe he'd been attacking me.

I swear, my arms were like noodles. If Mom, Dad, or Nana had been around, I would have given up and waited for help. Swimming was too hard. I couldn't make it back to the beach.

But I was on my own.

I kept swimming as a gull hovered about six feet above me. It tilted from wing to wing, opening its orange bill in a braying call.

He didn't care that I was exhausted and traumatized. Neither did the waves. Or that renegade sea lion.

If anything, Mirage Beach was welcoming me back with a reminder: Don't get cocky.

Amazingly, I was on time for work.

In my struggle with the kelp, I'd pulled a hamstring or some other vital muscle. I knew because making it up the Sea Horse Inn's steps was a chore.

Nana opened the back door like she was greeting a guest. She wore a cornflower blue dress that matched her eyes. She caught me into a careful hug.

"I saw you hobbling," she said.

"I went for a swim and I'm so out of shape," I admitted.

I thought it was close enough to the truth, until I

noticed Nana's worried eyes. I blurted the first thing I could think of to cheer her up. "You haven't tried my reading again."

But Nana didn't whip out the copper disk she used for scrying. I expected her top-secret smile and a promise to meet right after breakfast. Instead she shook her head.

"Let's give it another day," she said.

I didn't ask why, but I thought of her rubbing her brow yesterday. What had I done to short-circuit her divining powers?

"About our guests," she said, hurrying me into the kitchen.

"How nice that m'lady could make it," Thelma joked when she saw me.

"Don't mind her," Nana said. "Now, for brunch, we've only the Hellers and a Ms. Fortunato, who arrived with a Great Dane late last night."

"A Great Dane?" I gasped.

I pictured Nana's fine china, delicate shells, handmade beeswax candles, and a wagging tail as big as my forearm.

"Goliath is better behaved than Mrs. Heller, if you ask me," Thelma muttered.

"Which no one did," Nana reminded her. "Gwennie, since we have no other reservations for tonight, you may have the afternoon off."

"But Nana, I've only worked a day and a half!"

"You'll have plenty to do getting ready for Midsummer's Eve, and this way I won't have to pay you overtime," Nana said.

Pay? A *ch-ching* sounded in my mind but was quickly drowned out with guilt. I wasn't supposed to get paid.

"I'm here to help you, Nana," I protested. "Please don't pay me."

"And you are helping," Nana said. Her eyes softened and she touched my cheek. "As for wages, don't think I won't make you work for them. After tonight, we're booked solid. In fact, we even have a waiting list."

I didn't have time to plan my afternoon off or worry over the pain that lanced through my spine as I placed platters of eggs Benedict, home fried potatoes, and sliced fresh fruit on Nana's polished mahogany sideboard.

I limped a little as I hurried back to the kitchen to take the baskets of apple muffins from Thelma, but I returned before I heard feet on the stairs.

Guests were coming down for breakfast, and Nana greeted them at the foot of the stairs.

I glanced in the mirror above the sideboard. Using my hairbrush like a weapon, I'd pulled my wet hair into a high knot and skewered it with hairpins. I'd put on a blouse with cutout lace that buttoned halfway up my neck and wore thin silver hoop earrings. A few sand-colored freckles had shown up on my cheeks, from the sun, but there was nothing I could do about them. Despite my near-death experience, I looked okay.

The only sign that I'd nearly drowned was a faint red swelling around my right ankle. My saltwater-induced nausea had subsided, leaving me ravenous.

I surveyed the eggs, potatoes, fruit, and muffins and suppressed the urge to stuff them into my mouth with both hands.

Nana held court at the table, but she watched me while I poured coffee. What was she thinking?

When I returned to the kitchen to get hot water for Nana's tea, Thelma held out a muffin.

"Try this," she ordered, and I couldn't resist.

"Am I like the royal taster?" I said, but my words were muffled from chewing.

"It's not poison, if that's what you mean," Thelma said. "But it's not like her own," she nodded toward the dining room and Nana. "This is as it should be, with me cookin', you servin', and her as hostess. Still . . ."

I let Thelma talk while I savored the muffin. A thin crust made its tender inside, studded with cinnamon-spiced apples, even better. I could have eaten a hundred of them, but I managed to say, "It's wonderful."

Thelma watched me chew. She looked dubious as she refilled the china teapot with scalding hot water from a vibrating kettle. I brushed the crumbs from the front of my blouse before I picked the teapot up to return to the dining room.

"I know the boy you asked your Nan about."

"You do?" Not for a second did I pretend I didn't know who Thelma meant. Why waste time?

"His name is Jesse—"

Jesse. Perfect. The young-outlaw sound of it suited him.

"—but Jesse *what*, I haven't the faintest. He comes and goes, winter, summer—he's here, then not, and buys his clothes at the Merry Mermaid."

Maybe his parents were some kind of itinerant workers, I thought. Or, as I'd guessed, rich. Lots of people prowled thrift shops for bargains.

"Once, he ran with Zack and his lot. Not as much now, though, and that shows sense. Zack's turned bad, no matter how nice your Nana wants to be. Not bored, restless, or disadvantaged"—Thelma spat the last word—"That Zack, you don't want to leave anything weak where he can get at it."

I shuddered. It was a good thing Zack had brought out the pushy witch in me. What if he'd thought I was scared?

But I didn't want to discuss Zack. I had to wring from Thelma all she knew about Jesse.

A bell tinkled from the dining room. I flashed Thelma a questioning look.

"That should never happen," Thelma scolded. "You should anticipate what they want."

122

"But you—"

Thelma swatted at my skirt as if I were still about five years old. I hurried back into the dining room.

It turned out to be something I couldn't have anticipated, so that was cool.

Ms. Fortunato had been cutting a piece of cantaloupe, her knife had slipped, and her plate had skittered onto the floor. It wasn't that messy, but she was sure embarrassed.

The Great Dane, lying at the foot of the stairs, hadn't moved to lap it up, but I couldn't help wondering what he would have done if we'd been serving sausage.

I cleaned things up, and Nana told me later that my "no big deal" attitude was absolutely perfect. I'd made the guest feel at home and taken care of the problem, too.

When breakfast ended and a big van with a rainbow painted on it pulled up outside the Inn and tooted its horn, it was the icing on the cake.

"The bookmobile!" I cheered, and both Nana and Thelma laughed.

Because Mirage Beach was far from a public library, we qualified for the county outreach program. I hadn't been inside a bookmobile since I was ten years old, but it was as cool as I remembered. Sort of like a school bus, only instead of seats, there were book racks.

I used Nana's library card and loaded up on mysteries, romances, and a book of Celtic legends. That pleased the librarian. Tickled him, Nana said when we were coming back down the steps, since he'd stuck that book on the bookmobile as an afterthought, in anticipation of Midsummer's Eve.

Nana's walking cast got her down the bookmobile stairs more nimbly than my bruised ankle. And of course she noticed and insisted I take two aspirin with water. She forced a baggie full of more aspirin on me too.

"Have yourself a nice cup of tea and a lie down," she urged as I started back to Cook's Cottage. "Thelma and I are taking the rest of the day off, and so should you."

I wasn't the napping type, but I could already feel my eyelids drooping.

"But if other guests show up—"

"We'll fetch you," Thelma said. "Have no worry about that."

"Come back for dinner," Nana urged. "It will be simple. Soup and sandwiches, something like that."

"I might," I said, yawning. "Or I might sleep through dinner."

"There's plenty in your freezer if you should wake for a midnight snack," Thelma said, and I remembered the four-cheese ravioli Mandi had spotted in my refrigerator.

"Every night's like a party around here," I told them.

"Oh, yes, we're quite the lively crew," Nana chuckled.

I kissed her on the cheek and set off for home.

Already the cottage felt like home again. I checked

the hedge for my industrious spider, and she was spinning away amid the ripening blackberries. A subdued flutter told me the mother swallow was in her nest.

It took me a couple of minutes to find my house key. It had slipped into the lining of my skirt pocket. When my fingers located it, I unlocked the front door and collapsed on the couch with my stack of books. I'd just put two pillows under my heel when I thought I really should make sure the spare key was hanging on the cup hook under the kitchen windowsill.

I was sure Dad would have freaked out, searching for it, if it hadn't been there, but still.

Oh well, if I misplaced my key, I could probably get the screen off my old bedroom window and burgle my own house.

"Besides, it would be a shame to disturb the kitty," I said as Gumbo curled up on my tummy, purring.

I read until I couldn't stop yawning, and then I fell asleep.

Lightning and waves, sea lions, and long, tangled mermaid's hair wove through my dreams. I don't know how they added up to a restful summer nap, but they did.

I woke at twilight, recognized the quiet that signaled low tide, and decided I should go clamming for my dinner. I felt so relaxed and rejuvenated, I even believed it was my own idea.

APPLE BLOSSOM
(Escallonia langleyensis)

❖

*T*olerates full sun and heavy doses of salt spray. This sweet, pale pink
variety blooms through midsummer. Although at home in the most
traditional English garden, it may sprawl as if trying to reach the gulls,
broken shells, and rocks on the nearby shore. The careful coastal gardener
will take charge of this variety of rock rose, lest it run wild.

CHAPTER SEVEN

❖

Mostly, I'd be a vegetarian if I had to kill my own food.
Do I eat hamburgers? Yes. Would I look into a cow's trusting brown eyes and aim a gun between them? No way.

Call me hypocritical, but there it is. Except for clams.

Don't discuss their nervous systems or consciousness
with me, because I don't want to know.

After shaking the nap cobwebs from my brain, I got
dressed. With that aching thigh and tender ankle, my
jeans were a challenge, but I got them on, along with the
first T-shirt I touched. Because the beach cools off fast
after sundown, I tied my hooded red sweatshirt around
my waist.

I walked to the beach wearing a backpack loaded
with matches, a pocket knife, a copper-bottomed

saucepan, a footed rack to hold the pan above the fire, a little metal dish, and a cube of butter.

This was one beach treat I remembered how to make. Since Mom loved fresh clams as much as I did, I learned to prepare them by watching her during our shoreline cookouts when I was a kid, and more recently, when we'd driven to beaches closer to Valencia.

Striding away from Cook's Cottage I had one twinge in my thigh and another of loneliness when Gumbo mewed from an upstairs window. I waved and kept walking, feeling self-sufficient and hungry. It had been a long time since that apple muffin.

As I walked through the beach grass, I picked up driftwood. I snagged a few knots of sun-dried seaweed for kindling too, and breathed the salt wind which had probably blown it up here.

Down from the dunes, but before the bare shore, I saw sandpipers skipping flat-footed across the beach, stopping to root out dinner.

"Save some for me," I told them, then I knelt, built a foot-high tepee of driftwood over the dried seaweed, and set it alight. The sandpipers were probably eating little sand crabs, not clams, but my growling stomach made me greedy.

My fire caught with a satisfying *whoosh.* I built a ring of rocks around it and added driftwood, feeding the flames, and listening to the hiss of steam escaping from sticks that had looked dry but weren't.

Scanning the beach, I walked down and scooped a little salt water into my saucepan. As soon as I had done it, I saw the small rising bubbles and the first tiny hole, telling me where to dig.

I ran to it and used my foot as a shovel. The cold wavelets had numbed my ankle enough that it didn't hurt. Setting the pot to one side, I used my hands to feel for the hard shell, then plunged in, grabbed, and dragged it out.

"Ha! Gotcha!"

When the first clam plinked into my pot, it was like a starter's gun. I raced up and down the beach, kicking at the sand, squatting and digging like a dog until I reached each gritty prize. I scooped up a handful of long, leafy seaweed and stuffed it into the pot too.

"Don't worry about why," I told the clams, then pressed my lips together. It was a bad idea to talk to your dinner before cooking it.

I'd gathered two dozen clams before I settled down to cook. All of them were closed tight, "clammed up," you might say. I'd have to steam them in a couple of batches, waiting for each one to pop open. By then the metal dish I'd placed near the fire would be awash with melted butter. I'd dip each succulent piece of meat in the butter and feast on the freshest seafood in the world.

It was dark when I ate the first one, but there was a

moon. It was almost full with an iridescent ring around it. I tried to remember what that meant. I couldn't, but I did notice how the moon's sheen lit the waves as the tide began rolling back in.

Their crests blew back like manes on white horses. Poseidon's horses. He was the god of the ocean. Didn't stories say he drove his chariot up from his watery kingdom, grabbed unwary maidens by the waist, and dragged them back under the sea? Was that the myth or was I making it up? Maybe the story had been in that book I'd been reading as I fell asleep this afternoon.

I ate another clam. Because I was so focused on licking my fingers, it was too late to do anything when I saw him.

Black against the darkness, he came ashore. Bigger than the guy at the cove, I thought. I should run. Or stay very still.

Instead, I straightened my shoulders, lifted my chin, and tried to look intimidating. And then I saw it *was* him.

He'd stopped right in front of me when I remembered his name. *Jesse.* But I couldn't seem to spit it out.

"Hi," I managed. Didn't he ever wear a shirt?

"Hello," he said. His legs folded, and with an athletic grace, he sat—not on the other side of the fire—but right beside me.

His black hair dripped. Firelight highlighted his cheekbones, and I thought maybe he looked Native American.

"Jesse?" I asked, and the smile that claimed his face

told me Thelma had been right. "Since you already knew *my* name—Hey!"

He snatched one of my uncooked clams. Before I could stop him, he'd cracked the shells apart, bitten the mollusk from inside, and swallowed it. Alive.

Uncooked, the clam must have had the texture of rubber bands.

"You're supposed to steam them," I said, kind of aghast. "And dip them in melted butter." I demonstrated, and his expression flickered from confusion to disgust. "And asking if you could share would be sort of good manners."

What was I trying to do? I sounded like my mother! I wouldn't blame him if he jumped up and stalked down the beach, and I never saw him again.

But he only met my eyes and gave a faint smile.

"Manners," he echoed, as if I'd reminded him of an outdated concept.

"It's okay. I have plenty. Of clams, I mean. Help yourself."

Really. Is it any wonder I've never had a serious boyfriend?

Then I blurted, "Aren't you cold?"

He looked down, and I felt my own blush. Lucky it was dark. I mean, here's another humiliating admission. I'd never noticed boys have nipples.

"Your fire is quite enough to keep me warm," he said. As the flames glimmered on his eyes, he looked me over like a wolf sizing up dinner. After what happened to that clam—

As soon as the thought crossed my mind, he lowered his eyelids.

"I make you uneasy," he said. There was real despair in his tone. "How can I stop that?"

"You could start by wearing a shirt."

"Right!" That Celtic lilt filled each letter of the word, and he sounded as if I'd guessed a correct answer.

He moved closer, until there wasn't a foot of sand between us.

"I'm used to swimming here alone," he explained. "Around by the cove, actually. I leave my"—his head jerked up as if he'd heard something—"my . . . things . . . in the grotto and swim between the cove and the place with the boats."

"The harbor at Siena Bay?" I suggested.

As he nodded, his wet black hair curved on his cheek.

Why was that so familiar? I leaned back against both hands, pretending to stare at the moon.

"You do remember me now."

He reached out, slid his fingers around my wrist, and lifted one of my hands from the sand. I could let him have it, or fall. I shifted my weight forward, and let him hold my hand. He kept it cupped in his as his eyes locked on mine.

My stomach dropped like I was zooming to the stars.

Wind blew my hair across my lips, and he brushed it away. Not like he was grossed out that it stuck to my buttery lips. More like he'd wanted an excuse to touch me.

The ocean's foamy fingers crept closer. Waves moved in, brushing the shore.

Any minute I'd get it together and remember how to talk. Really soon.

"From the sea lion cove," I said. "I remember you from there."

"And from before," he said in a leading tone.

He released my hand so suddenly, I almost fell toward him.

"Don't deny it," he said, and flopped down on the sand, on his side, and then he laughed. "You remember me, and for some reason, it pleases you to pretend you don't."

It wasn't *pleasing* me a bit. I felt like I was talking with a higher being. Every few seconds I got the feeling he could read my mind.

"Okay," I said, crossing my arms. "Where do I supposedly remember you from?"

"Here," he said patiently. "It was later at night, and a long time ago. You were just a pup. You got knocked over by a wave—"

My head spun. Forget that kind of Western slang about me being "just a pup."

It was him.

The Gypsy boy.

He existed.

I exhaled so completely, it was as if I'd been holding my breath for seven years.

It was no big deal to him. He kept talking while I had a mental celebration because I wasn't crazy.

He wasn't an imaginary creature or a child molester or a dream formed as I'd sleepwalked across a lonely beach. I wasn't nuts and I never had been.

But I'd missed part of what he was saying, and I tried to catch up. Paying attention to him was the least I could do.

". . . habit of getting into trouble. Does it hurt?"

He touched my ankle gently, but he might as well have given me ten thousand volts. How could he know about this morning's tangle with the kelp?

"I noticed your limp," he explained.

"It's a little stiff," I said. Then I shrugged, and I must have winced, because he touched me again, this time between the shoulder blades.

"It bruised your back." He looked a little sad.

"Maybe," I said.

Had I been carrying myself oddly? I hadn't looked over my shoulder into a mirror, but my back ached from where the big sea lion had slammed me free of the kelp. It probably was black and blue, but I didn't want anyone watching me so closely they could guess my back hurt.

"I'm fine," I said as my excitement turned to wariness.

Even stalkers could be handsome. My dad could recite the names of dozens of sweet, helpful psychopaths.

I started gathering my stuff and putting it back into my backpack. I wanted him to leave before I started up to the cottage.

Actually, that wasn't true. I didn't want him to leave, but it would be best if he did.

I was about to douse the fire with sand, when his fingers caught my wrist again.

"Let go," I said. And he did.

That's when I should have stood up and walked away, but I didn't.

"You remembered," he paused to see me nod. "And you were nice. Then you changed." He drew a deep breath and looked confused, as if the change in me was his fault. "What happened?"

"Maybe I don't like being spied on," I said.

He thought for a minute. "That's fair. So what should I have done instead?"

This had to be a first. A guy was asking flirting advice from me. And really, raw clams aside, he was the handsomest guy I'd ever met.

"You could just come up and introduce yourself," I suggested. "Like a normal person."

That made him smile again, and I laughed.

"But I guess our first meeting wasn't exactly normal, so what could I expect?"

Grinning, he lay full-length in the sand, head propped on one palm, as if I were so amusing he wanted me to keep talking.

"Sure," I went on. "Just say, 'hi, I'm the guy who fished you out of the waves when you were a kid, and I've come back to set the record straight.'"

"I don't understand that part," he said.

Setting the record straight was probably a phrase that only existed in English. Where was he from, anyway?

"When you didn't stay around—" I broke off. Even by starlight I could see his grin fade into a vulnerable expression. "I don't blame you a bit. One minute you're skinny dipping alone, next you're rescuing some little kid from drowning, and then the beach is crawling with people. *I* don't blame you," I repeated, "but people assumed I'd either imagined you, or you were a bad guy."

His head moved as if he were starting to speak but couldn't come up with the right words.

"Of course, some of the old timers actually thought you were a selkie," I joked.

"And did you believe that?" He sat up suddenly. He might not know every twist and turn of English, but he seemed to know the selkie story.

"No," I said resolutely. "I think those stories were

made up by lonely women whose husbands were out fishing all the time. They put in the part where you could keep a man around by 'hiding his skin' because they wanted their own men to stay home."

It didn't feel right, mocking that myth. I thought of the Fisherman's Daughter story, of the dark, mysterious gentleman on the beach. If she'd hidden his skin, she could have kept him with her.

But that would have made a lousy story, I guess.

My story, my seven-year mystery, had ended. I'd accomplished my summer goal in just a couple of days. So why did I feel so frustrated?

I doused the fire, stood, slung my backpack straps over each shoulder and kept hold of them. He stood slowly, staying entirely too close.

"Why are you going?" he asked. "Let's do something."

I hesitated for a second. I shouldn't ask, but I couldn't resist.

"What do you want to do?" I asked.

"I don't care." He shifted from foot to foot. "I just want to be with you."

There it was again. *Jesse,* I thought, *you're weird.*

His childish eagerness made him unlike any adult I'd ever met. And he was an adult. Every inch of his muscular frame told me so and warned that an adult male with a boy's impatience would be unpredictable.

"Jesse," I said, heartily. "It's been nice talking with you."

"You don't sleepwalk any more." He tossed out the words like a lure.

That almost worked. Then I remembered I had only myself to depend upon.

In the waves this afternoon, I'd had to fight to keep my head above water.

Right now, I was sinking fast. I couldn't allow his charm to lap over me until I gave in.

"I got over sleepwalking," I admitted, making my tone quick and brittle. "Thanks again for not letting me drown." I hoisted my backpack straps higher.

"If it *was* you," I added under my breath. I mean, how dumb was I? How desperate for answers?

It was equally possible he'd just heard the story! Gossip that good died hard. I stormed away from him, fuming.

Of course! Jesse hung out with Zack. The guys had been shooting the bull about me, after the alley encounter.

What a close call. Wouldn't that have been perfect? The rumors would've gone on forever, if I'd let myself get tricked into believing Jesse—

The dunes reared before me. With all the sea grass waving, I miscalculated, and my ankle wobbled as I tried to stomp uphill.

I gritted my teeth against the pain. It didn't hurt that much, and I had to get the heck out of here. My cottage was a five minute walk away, and then I'd turn the dead bolt, latch the windows, and be done with this madness.

Wind was tossing the sand around and whistling through my hair. I don't know how I heard him.

"It was me. I don't lie."

I turned to face him and he was right there. Again he'd moved within touching distance, and I didn't know how. Through windswept black hair, his eyes held mine.

A long sigh deflated my anger. Despite logic, I believed him.

"I know," I said.

Few people realize I've never had a serious boyfriend. I try not to act like a total innocent. But the truth is, I've only had a few dates, and only one guy has ever given me a "real kiss." I hated it. When he shoved his fat sausage tongue in my mouth, I did not go mad with desire.

But right here, right now, facing Jesse, I felt a magnetism that convinced me we were going to kiss, and it might just be amazing.

I was so right.

His hands rested on my shoulders. I was leaning toward him when he met me halfway. It was a nice, soft, not at all spitty, kiss. I steadied myself with one hand on his waist. I was so spellbound that if my dad had suddenly appeared and reminded me serial killers were all this charismatic, I would have asked him who cared.

Suddenly the warmth that was Jesse disappeared.

He took a step back and gasped, "I would never kill you!"

"Did I say that?" I put both hands over my mouth. But I couldn't have. My lips had been closed by his.

"I'd protect you with my life!" His arms lifted skyward as if he were taking a vow.

"Wait just a minute."

My hands waved in front of me as if I were erasing this moment. I didn't want to, but I had to orient myself.

Mirage Point. Little Beach. Cook's Cottage just over the dunes.

I've known this guy for a grand total of—being generous and including that night seven years ago—fifteen minutes, tops. And PS, I don't even know Jesse's last name.

"You would not protect me with your life," I said, kindly. "You don't even know me."

"But it's true. And I don't lie."

"So you said."

He recoiled. I really had hurt his feelings this time.

"But even if you like me," I whispered, "you're sort of skipping about five million steps of courtship."

Courtship? Had I said *courtship*? What did I think, that this was Jane freakin' Eyre?

"I don't know what that is," he said, letting me off the hook.

"We're supposed to walk on the beach, holding hands,

and"—I looked around as if there'd be clues to what I should say next—"and go to movies, or go bowling. You know, listen to music together until we have *our* song. A pledge to—" My hands moved around each other like the blades of a lawn mower. I could tell I'd confused him even more. "—to protect each other with our lives . . ." My voice trailed off. "Jesse, that comes a lot later."

This time his voice was a growl. His hug knocked the backpack off my shoulders.

"I would do it." He talked against the side of my neck.

"No—" I said. His arms didn't hurt me, and I wasn't scared, but he wouldn't let me break away.

I closed my eyes. In the darkness, I still heard every word.

"We were meant to be together."

STRAWBERRY TREE
(Arbutus unedo Compacta)

❖

*A*s much a mainstay of the coastal garden as the summer romance, *Arbutus unedo Compacta* is a handsome shrub with dripping white flowers. It thrives in rocky places and puts on a show of red bark and strawberry-shaped fruits. Although these bright fruits attract birds, they are not sweet. Despite this subterfuge, in the language of flowers a strawberry tree conveys esteem and love from the giver. The strawberry tree should be planted in one place and left there, for once it is established, it cannot be moved.

CHAPTER EIGHT
❖

We were meant to be together.

Six words could make the difference between a madwoman and a sane one. I chose sane.

"This is crazy," I said and wrenched sideways out of his arms. Even though he let me go, I gave him a double-armed shove for good measure. "You're not going to turn a good deed—a *seven-year-old* good deed—into . . ." I groped for a less dramatic word than the one that kept popping up. "Oh, I give up! You can't turn chance into destiny."

His silence gave me time to notice cheekbones that slanted in a way I'd never seen before. He was exotic looking, no question, and he was having trouble understanding my babbling.

"Now, I'm going back to my cottage, and I don't want you to follow me."

"As if I were a dog, to follow at your heels." He sounded insulted, but that was better than hurt.

I kept walking.

Not until I reached the highest dune did I stop and look back. I saw his silhouette, all squared shoulders and blowing hair against the night.

"We'll speak of this later," he shouted, just in case I thought I was winning.

We turned away from each other at the same instant, staying even.

He didn't give up easily. I had to give him that. My sandals bogged down in the sand, but I smiled.

Jesse wasn't the first cute guy to try to play a girl. Trying didn't make him evil. If he went away because I'd confronted him, I wouldn't die. If he stuck around and tried to act ordinary—

I took a long breath and held it. I didn't know what I'd do.

Just ahead, Cook's Cottage showed its peaked roof. One loose shingle flapped a wave. I felt more grounded. Everything was normal. Except for that kiss . . .

My stomach was still doing flips when I woke the next morning. Maybe it was the clams. All I knew for sure was that I was about to be late for work.

142

I surveyed my bedroom, looking for something to wear. There was quite a selection on the floor, but the clean stuff was downstairs in my old room.

Once I got down there, I noticed the bike again. I leaned past my suitcases and squeezed the front tire. It felt full of air. Could Thelma have taken care of that, too?

Clothes, I reminded myself.

Even in my suitcase there wasn't much left. At the rate I was going, I'd be out of work clothes tomorrow.

I packed everything into a drawstring laundry bag, deciding to take them to Nana's and start a load of wash before breakfast.

I was feeling mature and responsible as I pulled on skirt and blouse before I fed Gumbo.

Moving fast, I slipped into the bathroom and pulled open the drawer in which I stowed my makeup. I guess I jerked too hard, because the entire drawer came out.

Moaning, I knelt to gather the little pots and cases, but I saw something that didn't belong. Amid the sparkly powder of shattered eye shadow, sat a rusty razor. Little bits of whisker clung to its blades. It sure wasn't mine.

"Ugh," I told Gumbo as she came to investigate. "I don't think this could be Dad's. I doubt he'd leave it behind, and I know it would be cleaner than this."

Shaking my head, I picked up the thing with a tissue, then threw it in the trash. Then I grabbed up the garden sign I'd lettered last night and raced to Sea Horse Inn.

I ran with crossed fingers, hoping no new guests had arrived last night. If they had, breakfast would start in about ten minutes.

In spite of my hurry, the twinge in my ankle didn't bother me. I arrived at Nana's with arms and legs pumping, laundry bag bouncing on my back.

"Gwennie!" Nana shouted my name before I zigged off the path to the kitchen's back door.

I screeched to a stop, like a cartoon car. I really felt good. I didn't care that I was being romanced by a crazy guy. Or a guy who thought I was crazy. I was still being romanced.

"We're on the terrace," Nana shouted.

I slowed to a quick, panting walk and checked to make sure the newly lettered sign I'd rolled and slipped into the bag hadn't smeared or crumpled.

Nana and Thelma were dressed in jeans, sitting on chaise lounges and dawdling over a meal of maple syrup–drenched French toast.

"Ta da," I said, displaying the new sign.

While Nana and Thelma read it, I collapsed on a step near them, wishing I weren't too lazy to detour to the kitchen for my own breakfast.

"That's for you," Nana said absently, indicating a covered plate they'd brought out just for me.

"Want me to fix this next to the strawberry tree before I sit down?" I asked.

Nana had a bundle of wooden stakes, forked at one end to hold a plastic sleeve, which protected ink from the fog and rain. I gestured toward them, but Nana and Thelma ignored me.

"It sounds a bit cynical to me," Thelma said.

"She wouldn't be her parents' girl if she weren't sarcastic," Nana suggested. "Besides, sarcastic isn't the same as cynical. Read that bit." Nana tapped the sign. "I'd say she's indicated that once a girl's heart has settled on a single beau, she won't be moving on. That's really quite romantic."

"It's not!" I told Nana, and reread the sign.

How Nana could ignore the part about putting out false fruit—like a guy pretending we were soul mates, let us just say for the sake of argument—was beyond me.

I shook my head and arranged the sign next to the tallest strawberry tree.

They were an unlikely pair of sunbathers, I thought, looking back at Nana and Thelma. I'd fallen in with a different crowd in the last three days.

I missed Jill and Mandi but guessed they were as busy as I was, or they would have called. But now I had something to tell them. Would Mandi and Jill just freak out if they saw Jesse and knew I'd been kissing him?

I tried to control the smile on my face but couldn't.

Although it was impossible to show him to them right away, I was pretty good with words. Maybe I'd give my girls a call right after breakfast.

I stood up, and checked my skirt to make sure I hadn't soiled it.

While I'd been squatting in the garden, Nana and Thelma had been discussing the guests who were due to arrive this afternoon. Nana planned to make dilly breads shaped like four-leaf clovers and some other things I didn't hear. Thelma was talking about laundry, bookkeeping, and kindling for the Midsummer's Eve bonfire.

"Perfect," Nana said as I stood from situating the sign.

"Thanks," I said. "Do you mind if I call Jill? I won't be long, I promise."

"Go right ahead, dear," Nana said.

The kitchen was quiet, so I dialed from there. I was getting way too big a thrill out of this.

"Hi—"

"Hi! You'll—"

"—is Jill. I'm either working or sleeping," said Jill's recorded voice. Then she sang a few bars of a song I'd never heard before about burning the candle at both ends. Usually, I would have hung up, but I just couldn't.

"Jill, if you were me, you wouldn't believe the night you just had."

I slammed down the receiver. That ought to tantalize her. And because I was so pleased with the prospect of

Jill calling Mandi and demanding to know what I'd told *her*, I didn't dial Mandi's number. Let them both simmer in suspense.

Smiling, I sauntered back to the garden, ready for my French toast.

"She wasn't home," I said to Nana and Thelma's expectant faces.

"You could've called the other girl," Nana offered.

I just gave a shrug that said, maybe next time. Then I attacked my French toast.

"Still and all, it's not what good Christians believe," Thelma said, obviously continuing a conversation I'd missed.

"Oh rubbish, there's no contradiction whatsoever," Nana replied.

Chewing, I waited to hear what came next. Their philosophical battle didn't sound new.

"Gwennie," Nana was trying to line me up on her side. I could hear it in her voice. "Do you believe in destiny?"

Like love at first sight? Like spotting a stranger among a throng of strangers at a street fair and having your heart swell? Like knowing his kiss is going to be the best one of your life?

"What I believe in, is laundry," I said, clanging the lid back on my empty plate. "I'll clear all of our plates on my way to the laundry room."

"The wet sheets are already out by the line, just

waiting to be hung," Thelma said. "Your Nan couldn't delay breakfast five minutes for me to get it up."

"Great," I said. Then I slung the drawstring bag of laundry over my shoulder and picked up all three of our plates.

As I headed for the kitchen I made excuses to myself. I just could not have that conversation about destiny with Nana and Thelma, even though I was anxious for that real reading from Nana's copper mirror.

Independence was great. I liked deciding on my own bedtimes and mealtimes, but when it came to Jesse, I needed some help. Not that scrying would point me in the right direction, but it might raise some interesting issues.

I rinsed off the dishes and shook my head at the suddenness of my feelings for Jesse. I was infatuated. At least. But he was strange, or mysterious. No, *exotic*. That word had crossed my mind before, and it still suited him best.

I slotted the dishes into the dishwasher, then headed back outside.

Though the laundry line was tucked into a corner of the Inn property, away from the eyes of guests, it still had an ocean view. Some people thought a laundry line looked low-rent. I was one of them, but the damp laundry smelled good, and I loved putting order to it.

I grabbed the first sheet, flapped it out until I found

the left corner, then fastened it with a wooden clothes-pin. I smoothed it taut to the middle. There I put the second clothespin just above the Sea Horse Inn insignia. Picked out in thick white thread, it was cameo shaped with a sea horse in the center. Then I smoothed to the right corner, where I made the first sheet and the next one share the third pin. And I kept going.

The clean white sheets danced before me, gathering the smells of summer, the sea spray, hot asphalt, salt, and Nana's pink and white flowers. Sheet after sheet I pinned them, border to border, tight and white.

Then my serenity fractured. I didn't feel alone.

Moving slowly, I leaned down to pull the last sheet from the wicker basket and cast a quick glance to see if feet showed beyond my wall of sheets.

None.

As I fastened its left corner, the last sheet flapped back at me, wrapping around my skirt, clinging to my bare legs. Only the wind, I told myself. I smoothed to the middle, then stretched up, pinning its right corner. That feeling wouldn't vanish.

Even as I bent to take the first pillowcase from the basket, the last sheet fluttered against my calves. I could have sworn a dark form on the other side of the sheets . . . Jesse's.

"Forget what I said."

Laundry hadn't billowed those words. Neither had

waves calling up from the shore. I'd heard a voice, but no one was there.

And then there was a louder voice.

"Have your friend come up for coffee," Nana shouted from the house.

I gasped and whirled, breaking free of the clammy sheet, and saw Nana waving.

She'd seen Jesse, so he must be here. I lifted the sheet in front of me and ducked under. I didn't see him, but all the sheets were waving. He could be hiding from me.

I moved between the rows of laundry, up and down the billowing white corridor as if I were pursuing someone. Where was he?

Finally I stood at one end of the clothesline. Waves thundered, a truck passed on the highway, country music swelling from its radio then fading. A gull hovered overhead, scoping out the white sheets to see what all the flapping was about, but I was all alone.

I didn't run up the hill to the house like a scared little girl, but I didn't dawdle. I slung the basket against my hip and went straight to the Inn. With calm precision I put the basket on its shelf in the laundry room then walked down the totally normal hall to the kitchen.

Nana's flyaway hair danced as she snipped dill weed into cottage cheese, making batter for her bread.

She glanced past my right shoulder. "Didn't you bring your friend?"

I glanced, too.

"There was no one there," I told her.

For a second her hands paused.

"Which of you is the shy one?" she asked.

"Nana, I was all alone."

"Must be getting old. I suppose it could be those wind-filled sheets had my eyes playing tricks on me." Her tone said she believed no such thing.

I swallowed, wanting to tell her I'd felt and heard whatever she'd seen. Even with Nana, though, I couldn't.

Besides, there was work to do.

"What should I do next?" I asked.

Nana ran through a list of things that had already been done—all the rooms made up, bathrooms freshened, and floors polished upstairs and down—and things that would have to be done Thursday, before the Midsummer guests arrived.

"You could look through some of the costumes and see what you'll wear," Nana said.

"Costumes?" Oh my gosh, this was going too far. I was a good kid, but I wasn't playing dress-up for the tourists.

"It's likely you'll be crowned Summer Queen," Nana said as if she were saying I'd stop someplace for gas for the Volkswagen.

I laughed, but part of me felt sort of bad when I did.

I'd seen photographs of Nana as Summer Queen. She'd been no one's grandmother or mother then, just a leggy girl named Elane, wearing a daisy crown, a Renaissance-looking dress, and a grin which rushed at you from the crackled surface of the black-and-white snapshot.

But heredity didn't mean I qualified to take her place.

"Nana, I know you were Summer Queen, but I'm just not the type."

"You are exactly the type," Thelma said, bustling through the kitchen with something destined for the compost pile.

"Just look at yourself." Nana towed me out of the kitchen to the parlor. Turning my shoulders, she faced me toward the mirror over the sideboard.

The me I saw wasn't as tidy as yesterday. Today I looked more like a beach bum, all straggling hair and sun-pinked skin.

"Auburn hair, green eyes—"

"Blue," I corrected, bugging my eyes out at her. "Nana, you know I have blue eyes."

"Blue-green," she allowed. "Anyway, you look a proper Celtic girl, and you will win the crown this year."

She gave a firm nod then walked back toward the kitchen.

"Why this year?" I insisted as I trailed after her. "Because I was too chicken to come back before now?"

Across the kitchen Thelma's shoulders stiffened, but she stayed put, probably because she wanted to hear what Nana had to say.

Nana took her time. Before she answered, she resumed whipping her batter with a wooden spoon.

"That's one uncharitable way to put it. But you're not a coward."

"I am, believe me," I told her. "I hate gossip and knowing it's about me. And even when I don't see them do it, I'm sure they can't wait to dissect my craziness later."

Thelma made a muffled grunt, but I could tell she was trying to comfort, not scold me, when she said, "It never occurred to you, I suppose, that folks have more on their minds than what happened to you seven years ago."

"I didn't say my feelings made sense," I said.

"But you're no coward, Gwen," Nana said without slowing her abuse of that poor helpless batter. "You faced your fear of sleepwalking. Now you're facing people. They're always harder. But as for becoming Summer Queen, it's simply *time*."

The word settled there like a stone in a puddle. I swear you could feel ripples coming out from it. And that spoon kept beating round and round. It was hypnotic, which is probably why I asked her.

"What did you see in my reading that bothered you?"

That stopped Nana's stirring and made Thelma head for the back door.

"Nana, I really want to know."

Her hand jerked away from the wooden spoon. It fell,

flipping batter onto the spotless kitchen counter.

"Then I guess you'd better see for yourself," Nana said.

She didn't clean up the counter. Instead, she slipped the mirror from her pocket and out of its pouch, then laid it before me.

She waited.

"I can't see anything but a kind of oblong piece of copper."

"Look harder."

"All right. It's bright reddish gold, mostly, but there are tarnished spots and smears."

"Harder."

My hands fisted. This was like being "taught" geometry when you had no aptitude for it. "I'm trying," I told her.

"Don't try. Look beyond the surface and the smears. Let your eyelids lower. Don't focus . . ."

It was like listening to someone talk as they fell asleep. I saw nothing, but Nana did.

"There," she said, but she didn't point. "The waves, the girl in the rain, and that"—Nana's voice cracked on *that*, as if tears interfered—"awful, blood-begotten storm. Blood and love and loss."

"You're starting to scare me," I admitted.

Nana shook her head and clapped her hand over the mirror. The gesture echoed the one she'd made two days ago.

"You see what I mean?" Nana asked. Despite her frustration, her normal tone had returned. "It's the Fisherman's Daughter legend and not your reading at all. Except around the edges, there are flowers."

"Like in your garden?" I asked, trying to understand.

"Or the crown," she said, nodding past the kitchen walls toward her own Summer Queen crown, dried and hung over the mantle.

"Nana, do you really believe in this? Do you think you're getting messages from"—I broke off, and my hand spun in the air—"somewhere?"

"Not really," she said. "I suppose it's all projection. Looking into the mirror, I see things I must already know on some level—forgotten memories or intuition, perhaps."

That made sense. Seven years ago, of course she knew I'd come back. Knowing I'd be seventeen, she might even have guessed I'd meet a guy. Although saying it would be a reunion was pretty shrewd.

"At least that's how it usually works." Nana shrugged.

"I don't suppose the mirror is high-tech enough to be broken," I joked.

"No, but—are you sure you couldn't see anything?" Nana asked. "Bringing your own insights to it could be helpful."

"Oh, Nana, quit!"

Thelma slammed back into the kitchen, propped one black canvas shoe up on a kitchen chair and retied her laces. I was amazed she was flexible enough to do it.

"I need you to do some raking," she declared. "For the big bonfires on the beach, we'll all contribute garden trimmings. I've left a rake just your size," she nodded to me, "out there. Just gather any loose bits of brush down toward the beach. Start in front and work all the way toward the back."

And so I did, wondering if the bonfires I remembered as a child could really have been so huge. Of course they couldn't. Not if people had actually jumped over them.

I thought of my auburn hair loose and a dress like the white one I'd borrowed from Nana. Both flying around me as I jumped a bonfire. How cool would that look?

Safety-Dad would have a fit, except he wouldn't be here. He was camping in Colorado. There was no way he could stop me.

I'd worked my way from the front of the Inn, back to Nana's garden. It was in pretty good shape. There weren't many trimmings to rake up. I looked down at the sweep of white beach. They'd light the bonfires there.

I stopped. My hands tightened on the rake. Daring the flames, diving from Mirage Point, kissing a stranger on the beach—where was all this outrageous stuff coming from?

Would I even imagine doing those things if Jill and Mandi were here?

I looked over the white shore, saw it meet the rolling waves and broad blue sky. On Midsummer's Eve the sky would be black, flecked with hot red sparks.

As we'd driven through Siena Bay we'd seen the banners for Midsummer Madness, and Jill and Mandi had promised to come back for it. After Jill got my message and talked to Mandi, I bet they would.

But what if Jesse stayed mad? After all, I'd given him a pretty good shove and called him a liar. Not to mention he'd thought I'd told him to sit and stay, like an obedient dog.

That had been my silliest mistake. Jesse was barely civilized, let alone a pet.

My mind veered back to the Midsummer competitions. Didn't the jumpers go in pairs? Didn't they hold hands?

I felt excited, then warm and lazy, as if my blood were thickening as I thought of Jesse's long legs and black hair, a little too shaggy. With him, I could soar over the flames.

"Sunstroke," Thelma said from the shade. "That's the only excuse for smilin' when you're workin' so hard. Unless you're thinking about that boy."

"What boy?" I asked automatically. Then, because she'd been the one to tell me his name, after all, I said, "Oh, Jesse?"

"That's the one. I was sweeping the upstairs hall and looked toward Cook's Cottage, and darned if he's not sitting on your front step."

I held the rake straight up.

"You did?" My heart beat out of control. "He is? How long ago?"

"Pret' near three minutes," Thelma said. "Long as it took me to come down and say it. Do you want me to take that rake, or are you planning to dance with it?"

I should have put the rake back in the garden shed, but if she was willing . . .

"Thanks," I told Thelma. I started off then looked back at her.

Thelma had lied to the police about seeing me on Mirage Point, and I was beginning to wonder why. If she liked me now, she'd probably liked me then, but there were lots of reasons for lying.

Sometimes you lie to protect people.

❖

*A*ttractive but deserving of its reputation as a garden bully, scotch-
broom self-sows aggressively, where it's wanted and often where
it's not. For hundreds of years it has been used for ritual witches'
brooms. Trimming back with a weed whacker may keep it in check.

CHAPTER NINE

❖

Just sitting on my step Jesse took my breath away.

His hands hung between knees canted out to the sides, and he smiled as if I'd brought Christmas.

He wore a long-sleeve black shirt, blue jeans, and he was barefoot.

"How's this for wearing clothes?" he asked.

I couldn't remember exactly what I'd told him. Something to do with me being less edgy if he wore a shirt. "It's great," I said. "But you must be too warm."

"*Clothes* are too warm," he said.

I laughed. He might be flushed from heat, but he was trying to please me.

"I want you to go swimming with me," he said.

"You didn't have to wait," I said. "You could have left me a note."

He considered his palms, then turned them down, examining both sides of his hands as if they were useless. "I can't write."

Every missionary impulse I had, flared alive.

"Or read?" I asked because they seemed to go together and because he didn't seem embarrassed to tell me.

"I can read a little," he said. "Signs and colors."

When he pointed toward the highway, I swallowed hard. Logging trucks loaded with five-hundred-year-old redwood trees came barreling down this highway. If you didn't read the warning signs, the trucks would surprise you. I couldn't drown out the imagined sound of a truck horn blaring.

"But *you* can't read eyes," he said in a pitying tone.

Is that what he did when he seemed to be reading minds? That wasn't possible, and yet I turned away, a little ashamed as I considered what Mandi and Jill would think of him. He wouldn't fit in—probably anywhere. But part of me—most of me—didn't care.

Jesse prowled away from my step. The nest over my head was silent as I watched him stare toward the highway that led to Siena Bay. There wasn't a car in sight so I didn't know what he was watching.

"Come swim with me," he said. "Now."

I would have agreed if he hadn't added *now*. I'd already gotten off on the wrong foot letting him kiss me as if he had a right to.

I wouldn't let him boss me around, but I studied Jesse and discovered I didn't want to fight him. Or change him. Why would I want to change a guy who took my breath away?

I liked the way he looked. I liked that he didn't act conceited even though I couldn't stop gawking at him. I even liked how he got his feelings hurt when I didn't believe him. He had some kind of integrity. And he'd promised to protect me with his life! Primitive, but it packed a punch.

With a scrape and a clang, a truck bottomed out taking a turn off the highway and onto Little Beach Road. My driveway. I saw a rooster tail of sparks where the oil pan scraped the asphalt and skidded onto the gravel.

Had Jesse heard them coming? Had he known they were headed for my cottage before he demanded I go swimming with him?

Raucous voices mixed with the cadence of rap, and I imagined they'd already been drinking. In fact, I imagined I heard the sound of beer cans, tossed in the truck bed from too many empty six-packs, tumbling around too.

Some movement in Jesse's neck and shoulders signaled a male on alert, like he was raising his hackles. He was totally focused on the guys, not on me. They had no idea how ready he was for them.

Then I recognized the boys from the alley. Zack, Roscoe, and a guy who, as he climbed out of the truck, proved to be a really strange shape. Roscoe called him Perch, and that's about how he was shaped. Wide, but like he'd been steamrollered. He wasn't fat from front to back, just across.

Thelma had said Jesse used to be part of Zack's crew. Maybe it was seeing him that made them look at home as they started up my hill.

But maybe there were other reasons. Like, they'd hung out here before. Isolated, without streetlights or police cruisers passing by, the cottage might appeal to them.

I thought of the wet footprint. And the rusty razor.

Jesse said, "Get inside."

His intentions were good so I didn't bristle at the order. "I'm not afraid of them," I told him.

Jesse gave me a frustrated look, but he didn't argue.

It would have been too late anyway. They were already there.

Roscoe and Perch looked surprised to see him, and a little uneasy.

That night in the alley maybe Jesse hadn't been hanging around with them. Maybe he'd been keeping watch over me.

But why? I meant it when I said they didn't scare me.

Perch might hurt me if he fell on me, and Roscoe had that little-dog attitude. I like little dogs, but it's as if they breed them down so that all of the nerves from a big dog have to be wound into a tighter bundle.

Zack was a little scary. Partly because of what Thelma had said, because I remembered the little kid beating his bike with a rock and launching an arrow at a sea lion. Partly because his shirt hung open just enough to show a really creepy tattoo.

A dagger pierced the vacant-eyed skull inked into Zack's skin. The words below it said, CRY LATER.

Zack must have misinterpreted my expression, because he was practically massaging me with his eyes.

Jesse stepped a little closer to me.

"Jesse," Zack nodded, forgetting all about me.

There was none of that "my man," hand-slapping stuff like guys do when they're glad to see each other. If they'd ever been friends, something had gone wrong.

Jesse's dark eyes touched each of the guys individually.

"Hi Zack, Perch, Roscoe." He smiled, then, as if he'd remembered that crack I'd made about manners, added, "Do you know Gwennie?"

I cringed. He'd have to start calling me Gwen.

"Me and Gwennie go way back," Zack said, and slouched closer to me, insinuating we'd been more than friends.

"We were both kids here," I explained. Then I sat back down on my porch, hoping I could just fade out of this drama.

"Who woulda guessed pudgy little Gwennie Cook'd turn out so nice."

I wanted to smack him, but that would be a bad idea. Jesse would pounce. I could see him watching me for a cue to jump all three of them.

Though Jesse looked stronger and smarter, three against one were bad odds. And I would bet they had knives.

I considered Roscoe's baggy pants. He could hide an Uzi in there, and no one would notice. Jesse's bravery would count for nothing against a gun. So I just stayed quiet, sitting on my porch, staring at nothing, as if I hadn't even heard Zack's leering remark.

Perch leaned into Roscoe's face and gave a burp. Roscoe reciprocated.

Forget the Uzi, I told myself.

But Zack's eyes looked dreamy. Maybe he was stoned, but I think it was an act to make Jesse relax. It made my nerves crank up even tighter.

"Jesse was here as a kid too, you know," Zack said.

This was news. I didn't trust Zack's sociable tone, but Jesse did. His killer stare turned friendly.

"Yeah, we bummed on the beach, *finding* wallets and spare change." Zack winked at me then his mouth turned down in a grimace. "He bought bait on the pier with his share. Anchovies, that cruddy bay shrimp, mussels, and ate 'em on our boat watchin' *Sesame Street.* Can you believe that?"

"*Sesame Street*?" Roscoe yowled.

"Yeah? You really got off on that baby show, Jess?" Perch asked.

"Couldn't get enough of it," Zack said, and then his lower lip protruded. "He was always too good to sleep over, too."

Living on a boat would be cramped. The television would be jammed between stacks of unpaid bills and a microwave oven. Food wrappers would be strewn over fishermen's boots and slickers, and it would be dark and smelly. Where would you do your homework?

And Zack's dad was rumored to beat him. I imagined Zack as that little blond kid I'd known, looking up as heavy feet crossed the deck overhead. He'd try not to cower.

Weak things aren't safe around him, Thelma had said, but she'd been talking about Zack.

"I don't sleep indoors." Jesse's matter-of-fact tone snapped me back to my sunny yard, but his thoughts had flowed in the same direction, because next he asked, "Does the old man still discipline you?"

Roscoe shuffled back from Zack. Perch licked his lips and gave a nervous laugh. Anyone could see this was something Zack didn't like to talk about.

"Discipline" was an odd word for what must have happened on that fishing boat. Making low wages, drinking too much—after all, Red O'Malley's bar hadn't stayed open all these years because tourists dropped by for cocktails—maybe "discipline" was what Zack's dad had called it.

"He hasn't tried for years," Zack said as his eyes narrowed. "Maybe you'd like to."

Roscoe elbowed Perch as if they were gonna have some fun, now.

But Jesse missed the dare. "Why? Have you done something?"

"Not yet," Zack said. He looked up as a shadow flitted overhead. "Hey, what's that?"

It took me only a second to notice the mother swallow duck into her nest.

With a cruel smile Zack crossed my yard and stood under the nest. I heard rustling, as if the swallow was sheltering her young.

It was easy to understand why he was acting this way. Who'd protected him, after all? Now he was tough and determined to prove it. But his memories of me were making things worse. I was the one—the *girl*—who'd hammered him with her fists and chased him up to the road.

Perch crowded close to the nest. Rising on his toes, he

curled one hand as if he'd flick the brittle mud nest, but Roscoe shouldered him aside. He reached into the pocket of his baggy jeans.

"Gwennie?" Jesse stood tall and tense, but I wasn't going to urge him into a fight he might not win.

I heard the snick of a match being struck and smelled sulphur. Roscoe tossed the match toward the entrance to the nest and missed.

Enough. I stood up.

Be cool, I told myself. Get hysterical and all of this stuff quaking under the surface will erupt.

"I know you're not setting my house on fire, Roscoe." I got right in his face, and he backed up a step then looked at Zack.

Zack glanced toward the Inn. My front porch was visible from there, if anyone was looking.

Without his go-ahead, Roscoe wasn't sure what to do, and then Zack just wandered away. He walked on the deck around the side of my cottage.

What was he doing? It took me a few seconds to decide, but then I followed in time to see him looking up under the eaves over my kitchen window. He must be searching for another nest, but I couldn't help thinking of my first night in the cottage.

What if the movement at the kitchen window hadn't been just my reflection?

Roscoe came around the corner with another lit match

then swore and dropped it when it burned his fingers.

Dumb as a rock, I thought, and this time Zack agreed.

"Put 'em away," he said, jostling Roscoe's arm.

Then Zack spotted my spider's web. For a minute it looked like he was just going to drag his fingers through the sticky strands. And I'd let him. He wouldn't try to touch her, and she could rebuild her web.

But just as I started to breathe, Zack took the matches from Roscoe.

She was just a spider, but I wouldn't let him burn her alive.

Through his black shirt I saw Jesse's chest rising and falling. He kept cocking his head to the side, trying to see my eyes.

I didn't believe he could read my mind through them, but just in case, I kept my back to him. I couldn't let him know I was scared. If he didn't notice how my hands were shaking, everything would be all right.

"Hey," I said, before he struck the match. "You know how Thelma and my grandmother are. They're watching me night and day. If they see fire here, they'll call out the volunteer fire department."

Zack shrugged as if he didn't care, but he shoved the matches into his pocket.

I thought they'd leave then, and they might have if Jesse hadn't come to stand beside me. I welcomed him, even wanted to lean against him, but I didn't. Zack's stare told me that would only cause more trouble.

Neither Zack nor Jesse said a word, but Roscoe scented trouble.

"Haven't seen you around much, Jesse," Roscoe said.

"Oh, Jesse?" Zack pushed a clump of shaggy blond hair back from his eyes. "He's a ladies' man now. Oh yeah," he said. Glancing at me, he must have seen I thought he was talking about Jesse and me. "Saw Jesse and Jade just the other night goin' at it."

And then Zack did this gross thing, grabbing the air in front of him at hip height before thrusting his hips forward with this disgusting, grinning grimace.

Jade? *Jade*, pierced and pink-haired, and too cool to sell me her earrings? That Jade? I turned my head slowly to stare at Jesse. He had the nerve to smile.

"Speakin' of cows, you shoulda seen the one we found out on the beach," Perch said.

I assumed Perch was talking about a woman, until Jesse got mad.

"At the cove?" Jesse asked, and then I knew they were talking about a sea lion.

You can't feel another person get gooseflesh, but Jesse was standing close enough that I swear I felt heat ripple over him.

Zack sensed it too, and he was smart enough to rescue Perch.

"She was already dead," Zack said.

Jesse's shoulders sank away from his black hair, and his muscles relaxed. I could imagine every one of those muscles, since he'd held me against them last night.

"I guess you don't remember, Jesse," Zack said.

He must have noticed my jealousy fading before he was through working on my feelings.

"I bet he hasn't told you what kinda here-today–gone-tomorrow guy he is."

"No, and I really don't care," I told him.

"This is boring," Roscoe said, looking around at my cottage.

Perch was going back for another look at the swallow's nest when Roscoe stuck out a leg and tripped him.

"Spaz," Roscoe laughed, but then Perch grabbed his ankle, jerked, and Roscoe lost his balance too.

"That hurt, man," Roscoe moaned.

Would they ever leave?

Every ounce of will I had was pushing them away. I think the only thing holding them there was Jesse. They didn't want to hang out with me, but they didn't want to leave me to him.

Once Roscoe and Perch stood up though, Zack started moving toward the driveway.

Gumbo picked that moment to jump up inside the window ledge and growl. All four guys turned.

Amber eyes glittering, she growled as she had our first night in the cottage. Black, orange, and white, back arched and fur fluffed, she was impossible to miss as she fixed them with a glare.

"What's that?" Zack asked.

"My cat," I said. I didn't try to make him feel dumb for asking. I didn't even want him looking at her.

"Does it come out?" Roscoe asked, rubbing his hands together. "Let it out."

"She's a house cat," I said. "And she bites."

Zack was grinning as he pushed Roscoe and Perch back down the path to his truck. Then he looked back and blew me a kiss.

We watched the green pickup drive out of sight.

"The girl named Jade," he began.

"I don't care," I told him.

I just wanted my cottage to myself. I wanted him to go, so I have no idea why I asked, "Do you want to come in for a soda?"

"I'll come in and see your cat," he said.

"Okay, but she's not very friendly."

Jumping down from the window and pattering straight to Jesse, Gumbo proved me a liar. She rubbed her side against his jeans then arched her back for his touch.

"She's a *nice* cat," he said reproachfully.

I opened the refrigerator, took out a cold soda can, and popped the top, then looked back.

"Sure you don't want one?"

Jesse shook his head then made himself at home. I'd never had a real boyfriend, but I didn't think they usually sprawled on your couch the first time you invited them in.

Still, I liked it. Gumbo leapt up beside him. He stroked her throat while she closed her eyes in ecstasy.

I could hear her purring from the kitchen, and I wanted to do the same thing.

Jesse's quiet strength had kept me calm out there. And if I'd whimpered even once, he would've beaten Zack bloody. I just knew it.

As soon as I raised my focus from the hand stroking Gumbo to Jesse's eyes, I saw him watching me.

"Come swim with me," he said.

"I can't," I said.

"Does your leg hurt? Do you have to work?" He teased me with my own excuses, and I guessed he didn't have to be a mind reader to know I was lying.

"I'll go tomorrow, I promise. I'm just not ready today."

He laughed.

You don't always notice the first time for things. Or the last.

Just as I couldn't miss our first kiss though, I couldn't miss the first time I heard Jesse laugh.

His full-out, rolling laugh reminded me of a wave smacking the shore then chuckling over small,

172

rounded rocks. Suddenly it was my favorite laugh in the world.

I couldn't stay away. I meandered toward the couch and looked down at him.

"You're always ready to swim," he said, struggling to sit up without displacing Gumbo. "You don't have to do anything!"

"Tomorrow ̄ "

He took my hand and pulled me toward him. I bent from the waist until our faces were just inches apart.

"Why would you put it off, Gwennie? If you wait another day it could be foggy. It could rain. There could be a red tide."

What was a red tide, anyway? Some kind of plankton die-off?

"That's not going to happen," I said, shaking my head hard enough that the braid I'd pinned up for work came bounding down and grazed his cheek.

"I could be gone."

The power trip, I realized, had just changed from mine to his. I didn't want him to leave, and he knew it.

"It's just swimming," he promised.

Oh my gosh. His voice was like melted chocolate. So were his eyes.

I waited for him to kiss me, and then I thought maybe he's waiting for me. But the moment had spun out just a little too long. Nervous, I bit my lip, and the movement was enough to make my braid wag. Gumbo took a swing at it.

I heard my own uneasy laugh as I stepped back.

His eyes still clung to me. There was time to save this moment if I only knew how.

"Where do you live?" I asked him.

Jesse's eyes turned wary. "Offshore," he said.

"Like, on an island? On a yacht?"

In one fluid movement he put Gumbo aside and stood. This time when he wrapped his arms around me, I was too aware that I came just up to his shoulder. Too aware that we were in my cottage alone. Too aware that I'd said no to swimming only to maintain a bit of control.

Jesse sighed like he was about forty years old. He flipped his black hair back from where it had fallen across one eye, and his jaw tensed as he gritted his teeth. Then with one arm still around me, he reached into the pocket of the faded black shirt.

He handed me a shell. I'm not sure what kind, though I'd once had a collection of hundreds. Hinged like angel's wings, it was cream-colored. Inside, a rosy flush was mirrored on each half.

As I stared he stepped away from me, then pointed at it with both index fingers.

"What?" I said.

"That's a double sunrise," he told me. "It says when

we'll meet for our swim. Can you be ready?"

I would have kissed him then, but he didn't wait. He stroked Gumbo down the length of her spine, opened my door, and jumped off my porch.

I rushed to the window and stared after him. Most guys would have turned back, would have checked to see if I was watching. But Jesse never would be most guys.

Sand crunched as his long strides took him away. His bare feet pounded the hot white sand as he headed toward Sea Horse Inn. Then, as I knew he would, he turned left down the path to Mirage Point.

He was out of sight before long, but I stood there wondering. Did he scramble down the rocky path to the cove or jump the wooden fence and dive into the sea?

Providing masses of color with a light and airy feeling, the Bridesmaid's cheeriness can be almost overwhelming to the onlooker. Still, its petals are useful for plucking in romantic "loves me, loves me not" tradition, and dreams of daisies bring good luck. The bridesmaid daisy self-sows with abandon, and though its wild profusion is short-lived, it delights the eye while it lasts.

CHAPTER TEN

Of course I couldn't resist going down to the cove before I went back to work.

I told myself it was because Zack had been here. Even unspoken, his threat to the sea lions scared me.

The path down wasn't damp as it was in the morning, so that made the footing easier. There was still that one slick spot, but I knew to watch out for it.

Seven female sea lions in shades of dark brown, auburn, and blond, lay on the sandy beach, pups dozing beside them. The big bull was there today. His battle scars and the pronounced crest on his forehead made him look fiercely prehistoric, unlike the females, whose eyes touched mine with empathy.

They accepted the bull's bluster because he arrived

with them in May and helped protect their pups until he left. His departure could come in June, July, or August. Only he knew when the time was right.

I still hadn't seen that big black sea lion who'd given me a hard-hitting rescue. For some reason, though I only glimpsed him, I'd thought he was a young male. If so, Bull had probably driven him off.

"Looks like you guys are doing fine," I said, and ran off to the Inn to face a full house.

Thelma greeted me with an accusation.

"The sugar bowl and the tongs have black spots," she said as soon as she saw me. "Do you know why?"

"Bubonic plague?" I asked, tying an apron over my shorts.

"Shoddy drying of the sterling," she corrected. "They'll need repolishing straightaway. Like this."

I got after it, soaping the pink sterling polish on an ornate knife with a firm, circular motion, just as Thelma had shown me.

She poured boiling water in each of three teapots, swirled it around, then dumped it into a spotless sink. She measured six teaspoons of three different teas into each.

"Slip into your dress while the tea steeps," Thelma instructed when I'd finished polishing, and then, pouring hot water over the leaves, she lowered her voice and began muttering.

I passed pyramids of green linen napkins bound with

shell rings on my way to change. Nana had set out the cream-colored china.

As I breezed back into the kitchen, Thelma was still talking to herself. This time I caught a few words:

". . . then will they offer bullocks upon the altar!" she said with a concluding nod.

"Are you reciting something?"

This wasn't the first time I'd noticed her doing it, just the first time I'd been bold enough to ask. It sounded like a Bible verse or Shakespeare, but I couldn't relate either one to brewing tea.

"Yes, and it would do you good to memorize it as well. Psalm 51 is precisely five minutes long, the time this tea needs to steep."

"The things you learn," I said as I carried the first tray into the parlor.

Sea Horse Inn had a younger crowd today. Five Tolkien fans from Portland, Oregon had come for the summer solstice. Three guys, two lanky and long-haired, the other a little pudgy, bespectacled, and paired with a girl who might have been his twin, and her sister.

From wisps of their conversation, I learned they'd pooled their money and were running this trip on a very tight budget.

The hungry eyes they cast on the tea table told me they planned to make dinner of the orange layer cake, the chocolate candies fashioned to look like turtles, and the tiny triangle sandwiches made of crabmeat and Swiss cheese.

I refilled the sandwich tray twice to make sure they got their money's worth, and Thelma supported me.

"It's nice to have some young people visit," Thelma said as I refilled the teapot. "This isn't Middle-earth, but the next best thing. Make sure they get more cake, too."

As I poured tea, Nana told stories, gently separating strands of popular mythology from Celtic tales.

I also met the Whartons, an older couple who listened as intently as the college students.

They were all having a good time, looking forward to twilight on the widow's walk with more stories, and no one made a mess, so I was happy.

I had a quick supper with Nana and Thelma in the kitchen while we planned Midsummer festivities. Nana got out another of her notebooks, which listed everything we'd do, starting the day after tomorrow.

I felt a little fidgety as I listened. I couldn't believe I'd turned down an afternoon swim with Jesse. In fact, I'd made a mess of the whole encounter. I'd done well enough with Zack, I guess, but I wish I'd made a plan to meet with Jesse tonight.

Zack said that Jesse didn't sleep inside, and Jesse had agreed. I wondered if that was true. Not that it mattered.

All I wanted to do was swim with him tomorrow, and

then if there was time, see if he wanted to come along when I drove into Siena Bay to gas up the Bug.

"There'll be lots of decorating and some preparation for the shoreline games," Nana said, drawing me back to the Sea Horse Inn.

"Tomorrow?" I asked, and Thelma's eyes flashed impatience.

"No dear, the day after tomorrow. Midsummer's Eve *day*."

"Of course," I said, and then tried to memorize my part in the celebration.

Besides decorating and cooking, I'd be called upon to dress in a Renaissance-style gown Nana had picked for me. If asked, I was supposed to embellish Celtic tales I knew for the guests or visitors strolling the beach.

"And then there'll be Dark Tea," Thelma said, looking a page beyond Nana's lists for Midsummer's day.

"The days will be growing short again," Nana explained. "So in honor—"

"In mourning," Thelma put in.

"Of course we'll serve our richest foods—curries and casseroles, perhaps some kedgeree. What do you think, Gwennie?"

"I think it's tasty," I admitted. Mom cooked up kedgeree on rainy weekends. Made of rice and fish, cream and saffron, it was delicious but not for the middle of June.

"—we'll draw the curtains, use candlelight—"

"Why do something so depressing?" I asked Nana. "It's like we're rushing through summer. I mean, I've only been out of school for two weeks!"

"Well, it is a centuries-old tradition," Nana said.

"I'm just thinking, if it's a nice day. I mean, it's sort of like with your garden. You work *with* nature and get better results, right? So why act like it's autumn before it is?"

Could I have been less articulate? It was embarrassing, the way I was mixing everything together. I was thinking of Jesse's *seize the day* pitch and my garden cards, and, well, I guess I'd just had too much time to think, being up in Cook's Cottage alone.

"Would you mind some company walking home?" Nana asked.

Oh my gosh, did Nana think I was going psycho? But Nana wasn't the lecturing type, so maybe I'd be able to explain my outburst.

"I'd like to walk along the shore for a minute," Nana said once we got outside. She was striding right along, so her leg must not have been bothering her. I guess it was possible my help really had done her some good. "The footrace will be here." She glanced up and down the shore and then stopped, smiling. "Look."

A cluster of rocks, furred with moss, held a single tide pool, and the moon's reflection shone there.

"The moon caught in a tide pool," I said.

"Or she's tired of all that vastness," Nana said, hand sweeping toward the black, star-strewn sky, "and wanted her own little spot."

I looked intently into the pool. I saw my own reflection amid the stars and rocks and silver dimpled moon.

Then for a single instant, I saw Jesse's face.

I turned with a gasp, but no one was there.

The Sea Horse Inn sat white-washed and prim behind us, but that was all.

"I thought I saw someone—" I said.

Nana waited patiently.

"Not in the tide pool looking back at me," I joked, "but reflected."

I pointed at the space between my ear and shoulder to show her where I'd seen him standing behind me.

"At Midsummer there are all sorts of fairies and elves about," Nana said. "Perhaps their invisibility is outwitted by water."

"Maybe," I said, shaking my head. "Or maybe I'm just seeing things."

Nana gave my shoulders a squeeze, then she stepped away from the beach, back toward the path. "I'm so glad you're here this summer, Gwennie. I don't worry about you being in Cook's Cottage alone, not even with that boy Jesse around."

That sounded a little bit like she meant the opposite.

Or that she wasn't worried about my security, but she was worried about sex.

"I trust you," Nana insisted, and there was so much conviction in her voice, I wasn't sure I deserved it. "I used to fret over your soft heart, but you've toughened it up. A bit too much, if you ask me. But it all comes with your concern over looking—"

"Crazy," I finished for her.

"You were never crazy." Nana stumbled a bit and grabbed my arm, but she didn't lose her train of thought. "Now with a little solitude, you're finding some balance."

I laughed. That was just the opposite of what I'd been thinking. Then after we'd walked a way in silence, I asked what she knew about Jesse.

It just went to show that what I told my parents was true. If they left me alone, I'd come to them when I needed help.

"Is he homeless?" I asked. He'd said he lived offshore; that could mean anything.

"I've asked around," Nana told me. "And he is a wanderer. It's natural people are suspicious, not knowing his family, but there's some admiration for him, too. Sadie"—she glanced over, checking to be sure I remembered my former teacher, so I nodded—"told me Jesse had a talk with a bookstore customer who'd left a dog locked in a hot car.

"Red says he's seen Jesse turn away from Zack and his lot when they're about to cause trouble. He's an upright kid, cordial unless others give him a reason not to be. And," Nana lowered her voice to a chuckle, "I hear Shawn McCracken's quite leery of him."

It took a second for that to sink in.

"Zack's dad?"

"Oh yes," she said.

I thought of the "disciplining" remark Jesse had made and the weird relationship he had with Zack. Jesse had no tolerance for cruelty. Zack seemed to revel in it. But it sounded as if Jesse had faced down Zack's dad when he was about to beat Zack. If that was true, I was really confused.

Our conversation had taken us within sight of the cottage, and I still had another question to ask.

"Nana, that night—"

"Yes, Gwennie?"

"Why did Thelma say she saw me up on the Point, when I was down on Little Beach? You know that's where they found me."

It was quiet for a moment. Waves broke, wind whispered through the sea grass, and I was so close to telling Nana what Jesse had told me.

"It's a mystery, Gwen." Nana's voice was as resolute as it had been when she said she trusted me.

"Haven't you ever asked her?"

"That would mean disbelieving one of you. Maybe you were one place, then sleepwalked to the other. Maybe she thought she saw you on the Point, and it was a wisp of fog. In any case, you didn't drown." Nana smiled.

"Jesse says he's the boy I saw that night."

"Ah!"

It would have been an exclamation, simply half of "aha!" except that Nana grabbed at her chest when she said it.

"Are you all right?" I closed around her, supporting her arms with mine.

"For heaven's sake, yes," Nana said, shaking me off.

As she did I felt eyes watching us. I didn't hear a footstep. Nothing couched beside my hedge, up ahead. And the moon was nearly full. I would have seen a lurker. But there was a dark feeling on the beach.

"It's a surprise, is all," Nana said. Then a few steps later she added, "But he's not like other boys, that's for certain. I would like to meet him if he intends to keep you company."

"I think he'd like to meet you, too."

We'd made it through my hedge, into my yard. *Sleep tight, little spider,* I thought as I looked ahead to my own cottage, snug and safe.

"Want to come in and say hi to Gumbo? I think she's bored with my company."

"I'd love it."

Nana sat down and, to my surprise, turned on the television. The reception wasn't very good, but together, we watched a scratchy transmission of the San Francisco news and gave Gumbo lots of attention.

It wasn't until Nana got up to leave that she mentioned the shell that Jesse had left sitting on my coffee table.

"It's lovely," she said. "Not from this coast, I don't believe."

"Jesse gave it to me," I said. "We're going swimming in the morning."

"May I hold it just a moment?"

"Sure," I said.

I should have known better, because suddenly Nana had that half smile on her lips, as if she were scrying.

"It's a lovely time, Gwennie. Just the two of you, gazing into each others' eyes, seeing all the best of each other, making one world . . ."

"Nana! I hardly know him. We're not making anything!"

"A lovely time," she repeated as if I hadn't yelped. "Don't let others break it apart, but don't risk too much either."

"Okay, but you've got me confused."

Nana handed me the shell. Then she scratched Gumbo behind her ears and dismissed her words. "I'm just a sleepy old woman who had best be walking home."

"Do you want me to drive you?" I asked, thinking of her stumble on the path.

"Pooh, by the time we get down to your car, I'd be halfway home," Nana said, and then she was hustling out the door.

Still holding the shell, I watched Nana from the window. She turned back once and gave me a wave.

I watched her walk out of sight, then considered the shell again, studying the delicate hinge between its two halves.

Anything could break it apart, because really, what was holding it together?

I set it down lightly, back on the coffee table, and went up to bed.

My morning with Jesse dawned perfect blue and gold. As soon as I opened my eyes I pictured him waiting for me at Little Beach.

I tied on my red two-piece, put my hair in a braid, and gathered what I'd need for work into my backpack. Just in case I was running too late to come back to the cottage to change.

I reached the crest of the last sand dune in time to see him swim around the rocks between the cove and Little Beach.

Graceful, quick, and natural, he was absolutely the best swimmer I'd ever watched.

I ran for the beach, dropped my towel, shucked off my jersey, and hurried out into the water.

I knew I was skipping my mother's shark-defense checklist, but I couldn't wait.

"Cold, cold, cold," I whimpered to myself, trying to get the goose bumps and flailing out of the way before he saw me. "Go!" I made a quick shallow dive and stroked out to him.

He waited, treading water, rising with each wave as it came up behind him. His black hair was slicked back, looking silver because it was so shiny. And I couldn't deny the way his face brightened because he was glad to see me.

I'd opened my mouth to say "hi" when his arms swung me around. Grabbing for balance, I held his shoulders, and he kept spinning us.

When he finally stopped, I was breathless, and the tail of my braid dripped over my shoulder. He was watching it much too intently, so I dipped lower in the water, letting the next wave lap against my chin.

"Yesterday I didn't come because I knew we'd be busy—"

He gave a "go on" gesture as if yesterday was forgotten.

"At the Inn," he said, suddenly looking precise and serious, "you're getting ready for the solstice?"

"We are," I said, and though I was still shivering a little, I told him about our preparations. "Are you coming to the bonfires tomorrow night?"

"Of course," he said. "We'll be the King and Queen of Summer."

"Oh, we will?" Why was everyone except me so sure of this?

He nodded. Even treading water he looked cocky.

"There's the footrace on land—that's your element, so you'll have to teach me what to do. And the swim—" He'd obviously given this a lot of thought, because he gave a piece-of-cake roll of his eyes. "You can learn to keep up with me."

"I'll have you know I'm a good swimmer," I scolded, and when I kicked out at him underwater, he caught my ankle with both of his.

Even though we were just playing, he moved amazingly fast. Really, if a shark had come after us, I'm certain he could have backhanded it away.

But it wasn't Jesse's quickness that made my stomach grip like a fist.

Once he had my ankle trapped between his, he slid his ankles up. To my calf. My knee. And a little higher.

The feeling left me speechless. For a minute. Then I rushed for something—anything!—to break this spell.

"It . . . it's the jumping over fire part that might give us a little trouble," I babbled, sculling backward in the water, out of his reach.

"It won't be the first or last of our miracles," he said smugly.

189

At least I think he said it. He could have told me by telepathy for all I knew, because we were staring into each other's eyes so hard it made me dizzy.

Falling forward, I thought, since the minute I'd returned to Mirage Beach, I'd been drawn toward the cove, toward the sea, toward Jesse.

And what had he said to me yesterday? It's only a swim? Ha.

"It's not an outright competition though, is it?" he asked. "Gwennie?"

Blurry thoughts came with heightened senses, I guess.

"Huh?" I answered.

"Isn't there some tradition of last year's Summer King and Queen choosing?"

"I think so," I had to look down to be coherent. I watched my hands make little circles under the surface. "And I think they're more games than competitions."

"Why can't you look at me?" he asked.

I can, but I might drown, I thought. But I didn't say that, thank goodness. I only blurted, "Where shall we go?"

He pointed to a sunny spot decorated with swaying kelp, and then he dove. I threw my head back for a gulp of air, not meaning to fill my eyes with blue sky and sunshine, but I took it with me when I arched after him.

He slowed and swam beside me. Currents surged

along our bodies. A forest of sea tangle opened for us. We were surrounded when he suddenly darted in front of me. For a heartbeat we were face-to-face, and then he kissed me.

Is an underwater kiss possible? Can you feel wreaths of bubbles floating through your hair, forming leis around your neck, and not gasp for breath?

I only know he kissed like an ocean god. When I opened my eyes, he was smiling. Then he took my hand and we swam on.

Beneath us yawned a deep blue underwater canyon. The sea felt thick, cool, and dark. The salt didn't burn my eyes.

As we started up, the green surface grew paler, golden, and then we burst through. Wind seared our faces. Startled gulls rose in squawking clouds. Sea lions rocketed beside us. Their luminous eyes flashed as we moved together toward the cove.

Had we swum from Little Beach, through the kelp forest to the cove on a single breath? Impossible.

"I can't believe we stayed under so long," I said, drawing a normal breath.

"I kiss like an ocean god?" he asked, and my heart stopped.

That thought couldn't have been spoken. I'd been underwater when he'd kissed me. Jesse's question was no random lucky guess, either.

He could read my mind. It was like being told you had to undress in front of a window if you ever wanted to change clothes.

I wished we'd stayed under water longer.

"Gwen? I asked—"

"I know what you asked, and yes, you do, but don't think it means anything."

He laughed, and a cacophony of seabirds flew up around us. I wanted to strangle him. I wanted to hug him. Underwater had been so smooth and simple.

I swung an arm over the water, creating a white wake, and I thought he was going to kiss me then, but he didn't. He splashed me instead and swam toward the cove.

"I'm not sure we should swim in there," I called after him, and he stopped. "If Bull takes exception to humans, it won't be pretty."

"Bull?" he asked.

"That big male sea lion with the jutting caveman forehead."

He gave me a superior look. "He's gone. Besides, he won't bother me."

"Well, he might bother me," I said. "And there's another one. A young male, I'm pretty sure, with an old cut across his nose." I took one hand from the water to make a quick slashing motion across my own nose. "He plays pretty rough."

I'd said too much. Jesse had already saved me from drowning once. He'd probably think I was accident prone, or a lousy swimmer, hearing I'd almost drowned a second time. But he'd latched onto another part of what I'd said.

"You're 'pretty sure' he's a male?" Jesse asked.

"The black sea lion? Yeah, well, you know. I didn't check."

Once more, Jesse's laughter sent seabirds scattering.

"You go ahead to the cove if you want to," I told him. When you were swimming with a tanned and muscled merman, it was probably a good idea to stay away from discussions of gender differences.

Still, I worried that he'd be hurt.

"Sea lions are at the top of the food chain around here, you know, and those teeth—" I shuddered. "I'm not chancing it."

His uppity look vanished, and he nodded with sudden understanding. "I think of danger when I swim along Mirage Beach. It's where I'm supposed to die."

"What? There is no *supposed to* about dying."

"Death in the green grotto," he said as if he were reciting. "That's where it will happen."

"How do you—Why do you think—?"

"I've always known," he said, and the spell that had held me in the kelp forest started to fade.

If he could read my mind, could he read the future?

And then he did something totally unexpected. He hugged me, but his head tipped down beneath my chin. His cheek pressed to my throat. He still held me up, but I was looking down on the black glossiness of his hair. When I stroked it, he sighed, and I felt this incredible wave of . . . tenderness.

Oh my God. This is like falling in love. I might *be* falling in love. But I couldn't. It was happening too fast. He was too weird and I was too young. Nothing made sense.

I closed my eyes. Sun sizzled on my shoulders, and I passed my hand over his hair again.

"Gwen?"

"Yes."

"You know why we have to be together, don't you?"

More weirdness was coming, I could hear it in his voice, but I'd stopped fighting it. I just shook my head. My chin skimmed over his wet hair.

"I'm your selkie."

"No—"

His arms tightened around me so hard, I gasped.

"Don't pull away or I'll take you underwater," he said in a totally normal tone. "I'm yours because you summoned me with your tears."

"But—" I kicked my legs and twisted, trying to see his face.

"Seven of them," he added.

Now I knew why he'd put us in this position. He

didn't want to see my eyes and "hear" what I was thinking. This entire day, no, this entire week—wait, my whole *life* was insane! But he wouldn't let me go.

"Jesse," I snarled, but that was as far as I got because he sank beneath the waves, taking me with him.

I came up, coughing, but Jesse didn't look a bit sorry. He pushed me through the water, away from him.

"Back to your Little Beach!" He dove again, pulling me along with him.

But he released me in a minute. Then my hand was free, and I saw the amber-blue bubble of him surging away.

I raced to follow because anger had turned to something else. Competition fizzed in my bloodstream. I could catch him.

My arms cut through the waves after him, but I stayed on the surface while he swam underneath. He had an incredible lung capacity, and I was out of shape, but he was *not* getting away after saying something so bizarre.

The muscles in my arms lengthened. My quads swelled with energy. My calves trembled, reminding me how it felt to bounce off a board, into the air, and tumble through the sky to slip smoothly into the exact place I'd chosen.

He was long gone, but I was so certain I'd see him just ahead, so sure I'd catch him, I swam past my landmark.

Realizing I'd lost him, I turned around and swam slowly back. When I staggered out of the shallows, I was too tired to be mad. My knees were so weak I thought I'd fall, and there he was sprawled on the white sand, basking.

I threw myself onto the sand beside him.

Forget the towel, forget the fact that this was a semi-public beach, forget the fact that he was certifiably insane. I let the warmth of the sun above and sand below seep into my chilled skin, and then, oh what the heck, I threw one of my arms over his back in a companionable hug.

He didn't open his eyes, but he made a groaning sound past an amazing smile.

After a few minutes, I pulled together enough strength to reach inside my beach bag for my watch. How long till I had to be at the Inn?

Jesse's hand flopped over mine, trapping it, before I could see the face of my watch. A gull with great timing laughed overhead. And still Jesse's eyes stayed closed.

"Are you sleeping?" I asked him.

"Aye," he said. Though I'd heard the Celtic lilt to his voice, this was the first time I'd heard him say *aye*. "And I'm going to tell you my dream, a selkie's dream." He must have heard me draw a breath to protest, because he said, "Just pretend."

And I did.

Face down, with the sun kneading my back, I listened as the everyday cadence of his voice changed to tell the story of a fisherman who lost his clasp knife while trying to skin a not-yet-dead sea lion.

"That's awful." I raised on my hands as if I were doing a push-up. "I don't want to hear this."

"Aye, you do," Jesse told me, and the gentle pressure of his palm on the small of my back lowered me back into the sand.

"Late that night a stranger knocked at the fisherman's door, despite the terrible storm that raged. So bad it was, the wind nearly ripped the door from the fisherman's hut as he opened it. The stranger pretended to return the knife, which had tumbled into the blue depths, but as soon as the fisherman reached for it, he was caught.

"In fact, the stranger was a selkie. He wrestled the fisherman into the surf. Then pulling him along, like so much deadweight, the selkie brought the fisherman up the coast to a quiet cove.

"There a grievously hurt woman of surpassing beauty awaited them. She was a selkie, and her mate, the stranger in the night, made the fisherman understand that only he, with his human hands, could save her."

Jesse paused. He lowered his face so close to mine, his breath stirred my hair. I opened my eyes and he stared back.

"I'm awake," I told him. "Keep talking."

"Right, well, seeing he'd hurt such a magical creature, the fisherman first grieved, then demanded brandy to deaden her pain, and needle and thread to sew her wound. But the selkies had neither . . ."

Jesse's voice trailed off, and I had the terrible feeling she'd die. The stupid human would've killed her, all unknowing. I didn't want to hear it, and I didn't want to be late for work.

". . . but needle and thread were not the way of it. . . . Oh, Gwennie, stop," he said as I tried to edge my watch where I could see it.

He flipped me onto my back and stared down at me. My heart was pounding.

"Don't go," he said, "or you'll ruin a perfect morning."

His eyes were so dark I could barely see the pupils.

"Are you going to tell me that tomorrow might not be perfect? Even though it will be Midsummer's Eve?" I asked.

"See? There are other things to learn besides letters. And you're doing a fine job of it, too."

I thought he'd kiss me then, too, but he didn't. What good was a psychic boyfriend, I thought grumpily, if—

"You like me again," he said, watching me.

"Oh yes, I do," I said, studying him right back, but my honesty embarrassed me. I jerked my hand free and looked at the time. "You have really made me late."

Jesse let me push to my feet. Then he rolled on his

side, leaned his head into his hand, and his eyes scanned up the length of my legs before he pretended to go back to sleep.

"So, are you going to hurry up and finish that story?" I asked. I wrung out my sopping braid, purposely splattering water on his chest. "Or will you keep me in suspense?"

I snatched up my towel, tied it around my waist, then gazed down at him, all sleepy in the sand. I was thinking about kicking just a teeny bit of sand his way, when his fingers clamped around my ankle, and, I admit it, I squeaked.

He gave a warm chuckle before letting go and rolling facedown in the sand.

"Keep you in suspense," he said, finally answering me. And even though his voice was muffled because he was face down in the sand, I think he added, "Tell me when you can't stand it any more."

❖

*T*ea *brewed from the petals of this wild pink rose inspires dreams of risky and passionate love. Sporting large fragrant flowers and spiny thorns, this strong and beautiful rose has been crowned queen of the seaside garden.*

CHAPTER ELEVEN

❖

Whether it was the extra work for the Midsummer celebration, or my failed reading, Nana seemed weary.

When I came into the kitchen, I noticed her paleness right away. But in the busyness of breakfast, I had forgotten until the guests dispersed and Nana was having tea in the kitchen. Her fingers wielded the sugar tongs between her cup and the sugar bowl so many times, I knew she was using it for energy.

"Gwennie, if you don't mind, I think I'll have you do my errands. There are just so many little things I've let go," she said.

"And those Hobbits kept her up, singing on the widow's walk half the night," Thelma grumped.

I knew she was talking about the Tolkien fans, but her words had painted an amusing picture.

"You did want to drive into Siena Bay for gasoline, didn't you?" Nana asked.

"Sure," I agreed, though my feelings seesawed between excitement and dread.

Anticipating my protests, I'm sure, Nana told me she'd left her list posted on the refrigerator. Then, for someone who was exhausted, she made a pretty speedy retreat upstairs.

I read the list as I walked home. The first item on the list stopped me dead.

Special fog headlights for the Cadillac, gleaned from a Los Angeles junkyard, could be picked up from Dr. Jack Cates.

No way, I thought. This was a setup.

"Nice move, Nana," I muttered. Of course I knew Dr. Cates was an avid amateur car repairman, but still.

Nana needed a bottle of lime oil, which I could get at Mrs. Leoni's grocery store, the place where I'd overheard, as a kid, that some people thought I'd been molested. The only errand which didn't require facing down my memories was ducking into Village Books for the new issue of *Tea Cozy* magazine.

I wanted Jesse to go with me, but the problem with having a boyfriend who had no address was that you couldn't find him. I didn't see him out on the Point. He wasn't down at the cove or sitting on my front porch.

A lot of cheeping and fluttering came from inside the swallows' nest. I wondered how long it would take them to learn to fly as I entered the door, bent to intercept Gumbo.

"Don't even think about it," I warned her. And when I gave her calico chest a gentle push, she actually hissed at me. "You have plenty to eat, inside."

Gumbo stalked away, flopped on the floor, and arched her neck to lick the patch of fur I'd contaminated with my touch.

I changed into clean shorts and a T-shirt, and I was out the door, headed for the Bug, when I finally remembered to check for the spare key.

It wasn't there. It wasn't my faulty memory either, because the little brass cup hook, under the kitchen windowsill was there, but it was empty.

I ignored the gooseflesh sweeping over me. I'd just have to keep track of my key, I thought, as I drove down the bumpy gravel road to the highway. I hadn't looked for that key in over seven years. The fact that it was missing didn't mean a thing.

Siena Bay looked better by daylight than it had at the farmers' market.

Since I hadn't spent any money all week, I paid for a double mocha at a little cart near the parking lot and drank it as I strolled around, surveying the bustle in the town square.

With card tables and metal hoops, tissue-paper flowers and fringe, booths were being made and canopies constructed. Midsummer Madness sales were advertised in each store window, but the square was beginning to look like an old-fashioned carnival.

I walked a lap around it, glad I didn't see Zack or his crew. But I didn't see Jesse either. In fact, although I got my share of grin-at-the-tourist smiles, I felt pleasantly anonymous.

Thelma was right. My childhood trauma wasn't the main thing on anyone's mind but mine.

I sipped down the rest of my mocha, tossed the cup, and headed toward the grocery store. I was adjusting the hem of my shorts when Red O'Malley appeared before me.

What was it I like so much about him? He was Nana's friend, owner of the Buoy's Club bar and a bait shop, but no more than that. Still, I was genuinely glad when he greeted me.

"Good morning to you, Miss Cook, and how go preparations for Midsummer up at the Inn?" He took my hand in his and gave it a few affectionate pats.

"Oh, fine," I began, but he interrupted, holding up his index finger as if he'd just remembered something I should know.

"Saw a friend of yours down on the docks."

My pulse kicked into gear. "You did?"

"Sittin' there eating bait, he was."

Jesse. In my strangest fantasies I'd never imagined I'd thrill to such a description. But that was my heart's response. My head was shouting that Jesse and I had a few issues to sort out.

"Now, there's some who think that's strange," Red was going on, "but I tell them, take those same mussels, write 'em up on a fancy menu as sushi, and you'll be payin' ten times the price as you do at my bait shop. That's why I say that Jesse's smart. Gave me the idea for my new T-shirts too. You'll see them in all the shops if you keep your eyes open."

"I will," I said, but I was already moving toward the docks.

Gulls wheeled and dived overhead, looking for a handout of deep-fried fish and chips from vacationers, or scraps from fish caught and cleaned on the dock. But I didn't pay much attention to anything except Jesse.

How long had it been since I'd seen him? Counting in hours didn't work for me. All I knew was that it had been way too long.

Shirtless and smiling, Jesse sat on the pier with his

strong brown legs dangling and his wet black hair sleek against his head.

"Hi," I said, looking down at the black mussel shells that lay empty on the newspaper they'd been wrapped in. Most of them lay open to show the iridescent blue and pink inside. "So, it's not just clams you eat raw?"

"No," he said, and as I settled beside him on the rough boards, he touched my cheek with a decidedly fishy-smelling hand. "Any fresh seafood will do."

As bad habits went, it wasn't awful. Some guys drank or kept tobacco bulging in their cheeks. Zack reeked of weed and preyed on weak things.

So, Jesse ate raw fish.

"I've been thinking about broadening my own culinary horizons," I said.

He studied me, mystified until I picked up one of the shiny, unopened mussels. Then he laughed. Do you know how many raw mussels I would eat to hear him laugh again?

I pried at the shells, but they were closed tight.

"Let me," he said.

Jesse opened the mussel and offered it like a ring box. I drew a deep breath then yanked the wet beige meat from the shell and popped it in my mouth.

I have no idea how it tasted. Salty, probably, but I was looking at Jesse. Weird Jesse, with eyes so dark his pupils weren't even there. Handsome Jesse, with his black hair dripping on high cheekbones and golden brown shoulders. My Jesse, who knew I was loving the sun's burn on my shoulders while I wished the world would stop.

If time stopped now, before Midsummer's Eve, before high school graduation, before Jesse had to leave, it would be great. That's what I was thinking, and Jesse seemed to echo it back to me.

So it's a good thing no one asked me how raw mussels tasted because I might have said something silly. For instance, mussels taste like love.

"Damn, I guess you just can't help draggin' people down to your level."

I recognized Zack's voice without turning.

Jesse ignored him and so did I.

He swaggered around in front of us, rubbing his eyes as if he'd just awakened, then shoving his tangled blond hair away from his eyes.

"I remember the time he got me to eat a razor clam," Zack said.

"He puked," Jesse said, but the words didn't seem natural on his tongue. I had a feeling he was remembering Zack telling the story some other time.

"Look at you." Zack looked down on me. "You're all clean and neat, but you sit down on that dirty pier, sticky with tar and fish guts, to be next to him."

Convulsed with disgust, Zack's face reminded me of

black-and-white photographs I'd seen of Ku Klux Klan members during the early days of the Civil Rights movement. It was like he thought I was lowering myself to be with Jesse.

He didn't spit at us, but I wouldn't have been shocked if he had.

When he trudged on down the pier to his job at the video arcade, it was a relief. Neither of us said a thing until a girl walked by wearing a T-shirt lettered RED'S BAIT SHOP AND SUSHI BAR, and somehow that reminded me I had errands to do for Nana. I must have jerked or something, because Jesse noticed.

"You have to go," he said fatalistically.

"I promised Nana I'd do some things for her," I said, "but come with me. Please."

He did. And this was more like having a boyfriend.

He held my hand as we walked to the grocery store. Inside, it wasn't scary at all. It was like going into a haunted house that had terrified you as a little kid, then going back as a teenager.

In Siena Bay everyone—except Zack—seemed to love Jesse. When we first came into Mrs. Leoni's grocery store, a cashier pointed at the NO SHIRT, NO SHOES, NO SERVICE sign on the wall.

As Jesse hesitated in the doorway, Mrs. Leoni appeared.

"Oh, it's you, Jesse," she said. "And Gwennie Cook,

how nice." She lowered her voice. "You two go on ahead."

You two. I liked the sound of that.

At Sadie Linnet's bookstore, a marvel of skylights, hanging plants, and fish tanks, Jesse had admirers as well.

"Just let me look at this a minute," I said, paging through a beautiful, big hardback book about the cliff divers in Acapulco.

Jesse fidgeted beside me. He couldn't wait to get back outside.

As I looked at the photographs I lectured myself about bravery. I should trust my instincts. See the spot. Aim for it. And dive off Mirage Point as I'd always wanted to do.

My eyes lost focus as I stared at the book. Walking around the village square, I'd spotted Dr. Cates's office, but it had been closed for lunch, and I wasn't going back. I knew the fog lights for Nana's Cadillac weren't crucial. In fact, I was pretty sure it was just a ruse to get me to talk with Dr. Cates again.

Well, I didn't need to talk with him. I was working things out on my own.

I felt Jesse's hand on my waist before I registered what he was saying.

"I'd love to see you dive."

I closed the book and positioned it back on the shelf, then looked up. It was weird how close I felt to him, when he knew nothing of my life in Valencia.

"I used to dive," I told him. "But not like that." I nodded at the book. "When I was a child, I wanted to dive off Mirage Point, but I always got scared at the last minute."

"Do it now," he said.

I raised up on tiptoe, and right there in Village Books, I kissed him on the cheek.

He left me just after that, refusing a trip to the gas station and a ride back to Mirage Beach. Jesse didn't like cars any more than he liked being inside houses or shops. As I drove back to my cottage, I sympathized. The roads around here were so rough, they almost made me bite my tongue.

The next day we were busy at the Inn, so busy, that I arrived at 7 A.M. and didn't get to go home at all.

We draped flower garlands, wove ribbons every place ribbons could be woven, baked trifles full of peaches and cherries, and iced King's Cakes to be eaten after midnight.

I wore a green and gold gown patterned with vines and roses. It was long, clingy, and actually easy to move in. I was just climbing down from dusting Nana's Queen crowns above the hearth when one of the college kids—or Hobbits, as Thelma persisted in calling them—hailed me.

The casement windows were open, and the Hobbits sat on the patio, talking and reading and waiting for the solstice fun to begin.

"I'm a recovering nerd," confided Arnold, the bespectacled one. "And I'm the only one who remembers your grandmother's way of telling the selkie legend *correctly*." He looked pointedly at the others before turning back to me. "Could you help me out, here?"

Blowing my hair from my eyes, I looked at the others. "Yes?"

"He's saying it's a local legend," the girl named Myra said.

I wobbled my hand back and forth.

"It's a Scottish legend transplanted here and probably Americanized a little." While I drew a breath, she bragged, "See!" so I tried to stay in Arnold's corner. "The word 'selkie' comes from the Scottish for seal, and we only have sea lions here, but if you look out there"—I gestured toward the beach—"it's clear how the legend started. Look at that, beyond the shine on the water." I pointed at a black rock. "There, where the waves are lapping up and over."

When they'd all made sounds indicating they saw where I was pointing, I asked, "What is it?"

"A rock."

"—sea lion—"

"It could be either, but it's moving," Arnold said. "I give up. Is that a sea lion or a rock?"

"Exactly!" I crowed. "The only way to tell is by watching."

They started to argue about what they saw, and while they did, I decided I must be a better storyteller than I thought. I'd been positive it was a rock, but it was moving.

"It's either a dark-haired girl watching us or a rock with kelp floating around it," one of the guys said.

I didn't notice which one because I was shading my eyes. "You see what you want to see with the reflections and movements," Arnold speculated.

I didn't see a girl. I saw a man walking through the waves, headed for the beach at the Sea Horse Inn.

"But the magic is in the skin, am I right?" asked Myra.

Blinking, I looked away from the glare on the ocean to focus on her. "I think by their very nature selkies are magical."

"If you steal their skins, they're helpless. They just pine away."

"Bebe," Myra said to the girl with the short, blond hair, "that's what I read, too. They come ashore to dance naked in the moonlight and get captured."

Arnold laughed. "Then they should grab their skins and run for it!"

"Personally," said Bebe, "I think the legend has a lot to say about the society that created it."

Fighting down my unreasonable irritation with them all, I pretended to whisper to Myra and Bebe. "The males are pathologically handsome. And seductive."

The guys howled, and then Arnold started pointing, stabbing his index finger toward the beach. "Here comes one! Look!"

It was Jesse.

"Yep," I said. "My own private selkie."

It was only a joke, but I felt brittle, like I'd shatter into fragments if I laughed.

As I hurried off the patio and down to the beach, I heard conversation. Looking over my shoulder, up to the widow's walk, I saw Mr. and Mrs. Wharton sipping iced tea with Nana.

I gave a hesitant wave. Nana raised her hand. And eyebrows.

When I turned back, he was right in front of me.

"Jesse!" My voice jumped a few octaves from his hug, as he closed me against his wet chest and dripping cutoffs.

Embarrassed, I pulled away even though I didn't want to.

He didn't seem to notice.

"I've been thinking about something," he said, jumping right into it. "That night on Little Beach, why were you crying?"

He meant that night seven years ago.

"I need to know," he said, and his need erased my embarrassment.

I didn't care that we had an audience. They were too far away to hear, and I was remembering the little girl I'd been, weeping into the ocean in the middle of the night.

"I was alone on the beach. I woke up there and—"

"You were scared and that's what made you cry!"

"No," I said. "I was afraid for *you*. Think about it. There was this guy walking out into the ocean, deeper and deeper, and of course I didn't know how well you could swim. I was thinking . . ."

As clearly as if he were standing beside me, I could see my father shaking his head at the radio, saying, "We'd better batten down the hatches and tie down the livestock tonight, Gwennie, a big storm's blowing in."

I hadn't understood anything, except for the part about the storm.

Jesse stood safe in front of me, and I took his hand.

"I was afraid you'd drown."

For a minute he didn't seem to process my words.

His head tilted to the left and he blinked slowly. "You cried because you thought harm would come to me." A few seconds passed as he sized up everyone watching us. "I'll just go meet your Nana, since she's beckoning us."

He pointed, and it turned out he was right.

"Come on," I said. He wouldn't say anything about being a selkie would he? About being hooked up with me through destiny?

Each step made me surer this was a bad idea.

Just the same, I introduced them, and I swear, some kind of lightning leaped from Jesse to Nana. They looked each other over, and smiles lit their faces at exactly the same time.

"And how was your swim yesterday?" Nana asked.

"Perfect," he said.

Oh my gosh, if she only knew.

"Oh," fussed Mrs. Wharton. "This is a rough and rocky coastline. I'm quite sure I wouldn't care to swim here."

"My Gwendolyn grew up here," Nana said proudly. "She's a strong swimmer and an exquisite diver. I've watched her compete, many times."

"How does a young person get into that?" asked Mr. Wharton. He was just making conversation, but the Hobbits came tromping up the stairs in time to hear, and diving seemed a safer topic than, oh, how we'd met, so I explained.

"Usually because their parents want them to . . ."

"But that was not the case with you, Gwennie!" Nana looked amazed.

He'd said a young person, not me, so I kept going.

"Then you train by doing trampoline and v-ups and jump rope, and you start with a bunch of different kinds of dives, then learn to specialize . . ." I babbled until their eyes glazed over then ended my lecture. "But I'm taking a break from competition right now."

"And you miss it," Jesse said.

The older couple gave indulgent smiles. Weren't we lucky to be so in tune?

"I miss it a little," I admitted.

"She could have been the best in the state, you know," Nana said, and Jesse actually nodded in agreement, though he knew nothing of the sort.

"And there you have it," I said to the older couple. "The totally unbiased opinion of my grandmother and m-my—" I actually stuttered.

"Friend," said Nana.

"Mate," said Jesse.

What?

Before horror closed my throat completely, I managed to give a sickly smile and explain, "He's British—and I'm embarrassed. So I think I'll go back inside the Inn and set out the tea things, all right?"

They all laughed and gave understanding nods, knowing the word "mate" was British slang for friend, I guess. At least that's what I hoped they were laughing over.

I left Jesse right there and ran down the steps to the patio. I was heading through the blessedly empty parlor and rushing toward the kitchen, flooded with panic.

When Thelma said, "For you," I had no idea what she was talking about.

"The phone," she explained, and I realized she was extending the receiver.

"Gwen! My poor stranded sister," Mandi gushed. "I know we said we'd be up there tonight for the village thing—"

The festival in Siena Bay. That's what she meant, and it sounded like they weren't coming, which was really lucky, since I had forgotten all about it and promised Nana I'd stay here at Mirage Beach.

But it was like reaching an oasis to talk with Mandi. This time last week, I couldn't have guessed I'd welcome conversation with her as normal. Mandi, who longed to live in a fairy tale, would have been much better suited to the last six days than I was, but I didn't tell her.

"Hey, what's up?" I asked.

"Temperatures," Mandi said. "Can you believe the twins have chicken pox, and I'm still supposed to take care of them? It's gross. I'm not cut out to be a nanny. I've been tackling them so they don't scratch and scar, and smearing on all this goopy lotion. I am ready for some adult company, *if* you know what I mean."

I knew exactly what she meant, and it was a good thing they weren't coming to the Siena Bay festival. It wasn't Mardi Gras, but it could get crazy, and Mandi's taste in guys could be awful.

"Anyway, we were coming," Mandi said, "and I even have a little surprise for you, but Jill has to close at the Torch tonight. Have you ever heard of anything so brutal? I mean, five nights a week she serves greasy snacks to these people, and she has to stay until 2 A.M., even though she'd asked for the night off."

"Mandi, it's okay," I said. "I'm going to be busy. It's sort of a work night for me, too—"

"Oh, I'm sorry," Mandi said, as if she'd brought up something tragic.

I pictured myself dancing and singing and jumping over bonfires with Jesse. I didn't deserve her sympathy. Luckily, Mandi couldn't see my grin.

"But we are coming up tomorrow morning," she said. "Really."

"I think tomorrow will be more your kind of thing, anyway," I told her. "Midsummer Madness in Siena Bay has a street fair and game booths. We can go out in one of the boats and—"

"That'll be great, yeah—Timothy, don't you dare pick at that scab!"

The receiver clattered down and I waited.

When she came back, Mandi whispered, "They were so cute at the wedding, in their little tuxes and bow ties, but now they're only sweet when they're sleeping. Anyway, we just didn't want you to be waiting and wondering where we were and all."

"Well, you deserve tomorrow at the beach," I told her. "And I think it's really cool that you're coming, even though Jill doesn't get off until two. Don't let her fall asleep at the wheel," I added.

I knew Jill would drive if she could keep her eyelids propped open. She was terrified of Mandi's easily-distracted driving style.

"And if I'm already at work when you get here, the cottage will be open. Just be careful not to let Gumbo out."

"Sure, but there was something else," Mandi said, and I heard her fingernails tapping.

Waiting, I watched Thelma give the King's Cakes a last layer of frosting.

"That message you left for Jill!" she shrieked.

"There's this guy," I said.

"All right!" Mandi crowed.

"An extremely *cute guy*," I said. "But that's all I can tell you right now. You'll meet him tomorrow."

"For sure?" Mandi insisted. "And he's really cute?"

"Absolutely," I said.

By nightfall bonfires dotted the shoreline. All along the coast neighbors shared cookies, roasted hot dogs, and passed around bottles of wine. Little kids ran up and down the beach with illegal sparklers while siblings kept watch for the sheriff.

Zack, Roscoe, Perch, and their gang would be out "helling around in boats," so we wouldn't have to worry about them. At least that's what Thelma told me, and since she and Nana were the experts on all things solstice, I hoped they were right.

Jesse had slipped away while I was talking with Mandi, but Nana had extracted a promise from him before he left. He would be my partner for the Midsummer's Eve competitions, just as he'd told me this morning.

It had been hours since we'd cleared away the last tea of the old year, and though we'd mentioned it was tradition to stay up all night, the Whartons had retired to rest up for the Siena Bay festivities. The Hobbits were chugging coffee in the village, planning to come back up to the Point in time for the games, which wouldn't begin until full dark.

Leaving Nana and Jesse on the widow's walk without me had been a mistake. They'd convinced each other we'd be crowned Queen and King of Summer.

I still wasn't too clear on how that happened. The competitions were games. From what I could tell, most of them involved wandering around in the dark, sometimes blindfolded, often in the waves. One of them was a swim though, and that revved up my competitive spirit. Finally, there'd be fire leaping. I still didn't have that part straight, but Nana swore it would be instinctive.

In Valencia running *away* from fire was instinctive, but I kept quiet and watched for Jesse.

By nine o'clock I was dressed in tight green leggings with an overblouse of what I guess was homespun cotton. Sort of gauzy and ivory-colored and it fell just to my hips. I felt more like Robin Hood than Maid Marian, but it's what Nana wanted me to wear, and I wanted to make her happy.

"What time do you expect Jesse?" Nana asked.

I sighed. I'd been doing that ever since he left this afternoon.

Nana had stood beside me as I inspected my outfit. Now our eyes met in the parlor mirror.

If I explained Jesse's problem with time, it would sound like an excuse, so I shrugged. "We didn't really set a time, but I thought he'd be here by now."

"Honey, just have fun! It's not the end of the world if you don't win—although you will of course. You have only four jobs tonight. Except for staying awake . . ."

"What are my four jobs?"

Nana held up her index finger. Her eyes narrowed as she recalled a rhyme and recited it. "Dance round nine bonfires by dawn, find fairy rings in the lawn, kiss a lad 'fore he is gone, and never this year be woebegone."

"I'll do my best," I said, then spent another hour pacing between the patio and the house, hoping to see Jesse.

At ten o'clock bagpipes played on the shoreline. Trifle was mounded in silver bowls on the patio tables. The Welsh Rarebit brewed by Sadie Linnet smelled delicious, but I couldn't eat a thing and I knew why.

I didn't want to share Jesse. I didn't want people looking at us as a couple, because they'd start expecting things. I accepted his random comings and goings just fine. Mandi and Jill might not be charmed by his odd speech and uncanny intuition for what I was thinking. They might just think he was weird.

"So little Gwennie's grown up, and she's got her eyes on my crown, is that the way of it?" A buxom red-haired woman caught me in a hug.

I had no clue who she was, but I didn't have to admit it.

"You don't remember me? Gwennie! I'm Shannon O'Malley—," she shouted over a chorus of slide whistles played by a bunch of kids. "Well actually, I'm Shannon Rice now. He's mine—," she said, tugging the sleeve of an equally red-haired man. "—and so are they—" She pointed to the slide whistlers. "I used to be your babysitter!"

Red O'Malley's daughter, Shannon, and her husband, Eric, were last year's King and Queen of Summer. As such, they got to crown their successors.

"Haven't you grown up pretty," Shannon said. "Now Eric, look at her. Just look. She's a redhead like me, and next to no freckles. Gwennie, every Midsummer morning of my life, they've told me rubbing my freckles with dew would remove 'em—and look. So don't go believin' all the rhymes and rituals they'll be telling you."

"Go looking too long for fairy rings up in the hills, and you'll end up with a brood like ours," Eric leered at his wife and waggled his eyebrows.

I'd barely regained my breath from Shannon's hug when her father gave me another. "And Gwennie, where's your young man now? You need that fish-eatin' Jesse for the games."

"Red, you old fool, he'll be here," Nana said.

"And where's Jack Cates?" Sadie Linnet asked. "He's supposed to bring that syllabub of his. It would be a good thing if he didn't though," Sadie confided to me. "Or I won't go home sober."

Jack Cates, the psychologist? Wasn't it enough that he fixed cars and brains? Did he have to go around serving that sherry and cream concoction too?

I was cursed, and that's all there was to it.

"I need to stretch my legs."

I started walking. I paced down Nana's garden paths, looking at the signs I'd posted. I strode through the house, looking at Nana's wreaths. They hung suspended, waiting for mine to join them. I lunged out the front door where the sea horse mosaic spun, singing to itself in the darkness.

Then I took a long deep breath and pictured Dr. Cates and Jesse.

My eyes popped open.

Dr. Cates, meet my figment. My selkie, actually. Certainly, no need to apologize. I know you all thought he was imaginary. Or a child molester. And now he turns out to be my rescuer and a real man, at that. Oh, no really, please, don't torture yourself with regrets. How were you to know?

My nerves settled. If Dr. Cates showed up, I would introduce them, because Jesse wasn't a selkie spun out of my nightmare. He existed.

I sat on Nana's front step. Pretty soon I'd be sitting here in the dark. Wood smoke, music, and shouted hocus-pocus wafted up from the beach. I should have been feeling fine. Even if I spent the night without a partner, I'd found my own magic.

Jesse existed and he remembered.

"But what if he is a selkie?" My whisper flickered out, a condensation of all today's sighs.

If I wanted to believe he was, I could find plenty of evidence. He'd walked out of the storm-tossed ocean, apparently responding to my tears. He could read minds. There was the clothesline incident. Even Nana had "seen" him when he wasn't there. And I had seen his reflection over my shoulder when no one stood behind me. Could selkies be invisible at a whim?

Of course not. I raised my hands to cover my face and shook my head. I could explain it all away. Jesse would never convince me he really was a selkie.

No, there was one way. If I didn't have to take it on faith, if I saw him change with my own eyes, then I'd believe. But he wouldn't. If that moment of transformation had ever happened in the history of the world, wouldn't it be so vulnerable and private that a selkie could never allow a witness?

When my hands dropped into my lap, there he was.

Jesse walked down the Inn's driveway, face shining at the sight of me.

And seeing him, my heart leapt up.

LEMON QUEEN
(Santolina chamaecyparissus)

With its sharply aromatic, yellow-button flowers, this plant has trouble staying in the background. Included in a bouquet, these flowers warn of false riches. Lemon Queen tends to get woody unless chopped back occasionally, but it never feels a thing. In fact, it thanks the pruner by rebounding with more profuse blooms throughout the summer.

CHAPTER TWELVE

"Your hair is so pretty." Jesse skimmed a fingertip along the crisscrossed mesh Nana had braided from temple to temple like a headband.

"Thank you," I said.

"Are you cold?"

"Kind of." But he probably knew I'd shivered because he was touching me. It had nothing to do with the balmy June night.

"What about my clothes? Sadie at the bookstore said it was the thing to wear. 'Piratical,' she said."

Jesse, you're perfect, I thought, but I considered the black leggings and the flowing white shirt. "Do you think you'll be able to swim?"

"Of course."

Then the front porch light went off. It must be eleven o'clock.

Why did the darkness make the smell of Nana's violets so much sweeter? When I couldn't see her, why did the stone maiden pouring water into the goldfish pond make a more musical gurgle?

But the dousing of the lights didn't happen at Jesse's command. Nana had decreed no artificial lights after eleven o'clock.

I took Jesse's hand and led him into the Inn. "Let's cut through to the beach."

Candle wax and potpourri mixed with sea scents blowing through the open casement doors. Even in the darkness we swerved around furniture, headed for the patio, without running into anything.

Jesse didn't linger or hug me in a secret corner. He hurried.

Still holding hands, we walked down the grassy hill sloping to the packed sand bordering the waves. There were two bonfires on Sea Horse Inn grounds—a really big one, smelling of fruitwood and flowers, and another, which had been built right at the margin of the waves.

I hoped that was the one we were going to jump.

Tourists had gathered on the beach now, twenty or thirty of them, playing kazoos and singing in off-key voices. Many carried flashlights and wore hats. Cowboy hats, a horned Viking helmet, a drooping fool's cap.

The rowdy merrymakers included some townspeople, too.

A girl I'd seen before wore a belly dancer's bare-midriffed costume. She did a grapevining step around the bonfire, eyes fixed on Jesse. Her pinkish hair and heavily kohled eyes made her familiar.

"Let's go watch Red play the bagpipes," I said, but when Jesse slowed, I asked, "Do you know her?"

"She was in the village," Jesse said as I strode on. "She offered me some grog from a cauldron in the square."

"I just bet she did," I grumbled.

". . . and don't forget to gaze through the flames at your lover to see his true face," Sadie was telling some people in hiking boots.

Then everyone hushed at the bagpipe's skirl.

Red wore a tartan kilt and a plaid fastened at his left shoulder. It was easy to overlook his knobby old-man knees and everyday orneriness while he played. He cradled the leather bag as if it were a child, and though I doubt anyone knew the song, they watched, faces turned amber by firelight, falling under a spell.

"Gwennie," Jesse pulled me against his side, arm around my waist, but it was the music that held him transfixed. His eyes widened and he leaned forward. When Gina Leoni joined in, playing a silver flute, which looked tiny in her hands, his face shone with appreciation.

And then we were swept up by hands grabbing for ours.

"Circle of arms, circle of strife, circle of blooms, circle of life."

The chant went on, the same words over and over, reminding people that Midsummer meant both change and continuity.

We danced around one bonfire and then the next. *Two down and seven to go,* I thought. And I gazed down the black beach, seeing dozens of them, burning like pagan midnight suns as far as I could see.

"Eat these!" Some girl I'd never met closed my hand around something grainy, then did the same to Jesse. "Fern seeds to make you invisible!"

With her wide skirt bumping those around her, she flounced on down the beach.

"In the city I wouldn't think of eating these," I told Jesse. "But here . . ."

"Wouldn't you like to be invisible?" he asked.

But then Nana was at my side. "Poppy seeds," she told me, and then I turned to listen to Sadie telling the Hobbits about the solstice fires.

"In the earliest days, the fires were lit to warm the sun as it traveled on its winter journey, and some thought the height of the flames told the old gods our high hopes for our crops, or the size of the fishing catches we expected . . ."

"It's time for the race, Gwennie." Shannon appeared out of the crowd, carrying a fistful of white cloth.

It turned out that all the men were gathered at one end of the beach and all the women at the other. Once the competitors were blindfolded, they had to find each other. Only one each could they shout, "King, King, come to your Queen."

Before we parted, Jesse squeezed my hand. "See you in a minute."

Blatting horns and fluttering ribbons marked the starting line down the beach, and all of us made our barefooted way to it. Nana kissed me as I passed.

"We are *so* going to win," I told her, full of Jesse's confidence. "You'll have another crown for the mantel."

Once I reached the starting line with the other women, we were informed that we not only had to run blindfolded, but also had to have our thumbs tied behind our backs. A tide of laughter united us as we listened for the rest of the rules.

The men would have their hands free, and their job was to untie our thumbs and run with us back to their starting line. The first couple across, won.

Just before we were all blindfolded, we saw a little girl in a princess dress who would wave a wand and set us running with some magic word.

"Go!" she shouted, and there was more laughter until we were reminded the run must be silent.

Underfoot, the wet sand felt terrific. Shoulders jostled against each other, and the scents of lavender, soap, and perfumes of every kind came together.

We could hear the men's heavy footsteps approach. First one, then a dozen voices called out, "King, King, come to your queen," and then giggles filled the silence.

"I'm here," said Jesse's voice before I could call him, and he untied my thumbs, removed my blindfold, and led me running, but not toward the finish line.

We splashed into the waves.

"I think we should get used to it," he said. "Swimming's the race we want to win."

Every competitive bone in my body protested, but I didn't really care if we won. Not that much. I cared about standing in the waves, holding Jesse's hand.

Before the swim there was a tug-o-war over the water, and though we didn't join in, we watched.

Before we could begin the swimming race, we had to wait for Shannon's husband, Eric, who'd stubbed his toe on a rock.

After five minutes of hopping and moaning, Eric recovered, and we all lined up knee-deep in the sea.

I glanced over at Jesse just as Gina Leoni's flute signaled "Go!"

Together we flew forward lined out in flat racing dives into the sea. The sound of belly-flops splashed behind us.

He matched me stroke for stroke. Each time I raised my dripping face, I saw his. My hands looked small parting the waters beside his. Instead of diving and darting, he stayed next to me until we reached the marker boat.

Its candle-lantern glazed the ocean, turning the drops of salt water on Jesse's eyelashes gold. A warm gust of wind assisted our turn, and then the magic dropped away.

I felt fingers ripping the water at my toes.

"Faster!" Jesse ordered.

It was a point of honor, I could feel it. He could have tolerated losing the footrace. But he would not be beaten here.

Riptides are ruthless, and Jesse created his own, ducking me under the surface before I'd snatched a full breath. The glow of the finish-line lantern made a shifting beam above us. We followed it through salt water, then finally burst the surface. For an instant I thought his energy would take him vaulting over the rowboat, headfirst, arching like a seal.

It didn't, of course, but I tackled him, and we met in a soaked hug before we slogged ashore. My wet blouse dragged against my arms. I staggered a step, feeling my bruised ankle for the first time all night.

"Are you all right?" Jesse's arm went around me, warm through the wet fabric.

"I'm fine if you don't count how loony we both are to attempt that jump!"

There was the small bonfire before us, and it wasn't that small.

Now that all of us stood shivering, staring at it, I felt glad our clothes were wet. We might not be so combustible. A good thing, too, that we got a running start from the shore and leapt into the sea. That might put out any trailing flames.

Just do it, I told myself. Like each dive I'd tried for the first time, this one was a leap of faith. And I had something really good going for me this time. I didn't care about winning.

"Farther," I said when Jesse wanted to stop just a few yards from the fire. We backed up for a longer running start.

"All right?" he asked as I ran in place with eyes fixed on the flames.

"Almost," I said, but then he took my cheeks between his hands and looked into my eyes.

"Now?" he asked, grinning, and I nodded.

There was a moment as we ran, feet beating hard wet sand, stretching taller as we neared the red-orange heart of the fire, that I thought we were either going down in flames or soaring together.

Before we counted *one, two, three,* as planned, we were flying through a veil of heat and golden sparks. Air whistled. Waves crashed around us. We went under, then bolted to our feet.

We whirled and splashed, exulting and entwined, until the crowd dragged us ashore for the crowning.

After that there was no time to think.

It took only minutes. Pagans aren't much for waiting, I guess.

No one had warned me the celebration ended with a kind of wedding. They gave us each a garland and told us what to say.

"I crown thee King of Summer," I said, and the circlet of intertwined leaves and flowers I placed on Jesse's head slipped to one side on his wet black hair.

"I claim thee Queen of Summer," he said.

I gazed through my wet ribbons and tangled hair as Red O'Malley played a jig on his fiddle, and Jesse kissed me.

There was more dancing around the bonfire, more congratulations and hugs. We toasted and were fed King Cakes.

Flushed with triumph and heat from the bonfire, I couldn't help thinking of the fertility rites linked with the solstice. Rolling in the dew. Staying up all night. And we'd just been crowned summer's last couple.

I looked past the Inn, past the highway to the dark, grassy hills beyond. You could pretty much guess where this had led in the old days.

But not tonight. Some people began drifting toward home. Quiet settled, and the big bonfires made a crackling background for Nana's stories.

Red rubbed his eyes like a sleepy toddler, though Nana claimed he'd tend the bonfires till dawn. Jesse and I slipped past him to stare into the embers of the fire we considered ours.

Backs turned to the others, my arms circled Jesse's waist, and his locked around mine. We hadn't spoken for minutes. With my head leaned against his shoulder, I tried to figure out if it was my heartbeat or Jesse's that rocked me.

Then a voice sliced through the magic.

"Oh my God, will you look at Gwen!" A shrill laugh spiraled so that everyone on the beach heard it.

That quick, I felt stupid in my wet blouse, dripping ribbons, and cold feet. I unwound Jesse's arm from my waist and whipped the garland off my head. I shoved it toward Nana and went to meet Mandi and Jill.

My two worlds were colliding, and I wasn't sure what to do. One thing I couldn't do was leave Jesse behind. I forked my fingers through his, squeezed, then took a deep breath. I had the weirdest feeling that if I'd tried now, there was no way in the world I could have leapt over that fire.

"Is that one of your friends?" Jesse asked as he walked beside me.

For a minute I didn't want to claim her. Mandi had found the guy least likely to transform into a fairy-tale prince. She meandered down the beach from Cook's Cottage with Zack.

"Yeah," I managed.

"Does she know Zack?"

"I guess she does now."

Both shaggy and blond, they clung to each other, making a bad job of walking on the sand. Zack wore ripped jeans and a T-shirt stained with wine. Even from here he smelled like weed.

Mandi, in a magenta tube top and jeans, had had her share to drink, too, but she held to him like a prize.

A few steps behind, Perch and Roscoe dodged at Jill's heels, hoping to get lucky. Jill made an impatient, shooing movement that said they were dreaming.

"Hey, hon, come give me a hug," Jill called. Her arms dropped when I got within reach and she saw how soaked I was.

"Maybe not, I'm pretty wet," I said, making the excuse for her. Besides, I didn't want to release Jesse's hand.

Jill studied the two of us, and it didn't take her long to figure out I hadn't been expecting her tonight. She made an apologetic grimace.

"I got off early and we stopped in—" She made a vague gesture.

"Siena Bay?" I guessed.

"Right. There was a band in the square, and Mandi got to dancing and stuff, and, well, you know how she never forgets a face. She spotted the guy we saw in the green truck when we were driving through last weekend—"

Had it just been last weekend? Their lives had gone on as usual. Mine had spun out of control in a wonderful way. Except for Zack.

Even drunk, he was gloating. Watching me, he rubbed his hand along Mandi's hip, where her jeans were too low and her tube top too high.

If I said anything, the situation would only get worse. Besides, I noticed Jill was letting herself have a real eyeful of Jesse. His white shirt hung open at the throat, and his weight rested on one leg. With his garland askew, he looked like a disheveled Shakespearean actor. Clever and irresistible.

I was smiling when I glanced back at Jill.

Her eyebrows were arched up into her bangs. I had no idea what she was thinking.

"This is Jesse," I introduced him.

"He *is* pretty cute," Mandi said, shrugging from under Zack's arm. She hitched up her tube top as she approached.

Mandi was completely wasted. Everyone on the beach could see it.

As she leaned over, trying to get her toes back through the flip-flop on her right foot, she watched Jesse to see if he was checking out her cleavage.

Jesse wasn't looking. I knew, because he'd turned to

me instead. Just as he'd listened to my advice on wearing clothes, he was waiting for some tips on how to regard my drunken friend. This time I couldn't imagine what to tell him.

"So, like it's a lot more fun back in the village," Mandi announced.

"A *lot* more fun," Zack echoed, then bent her backward for a sloppy kiss.

Jill gave an eye roll of disgust. We needed to get Mandi out of here for her own good, but I didn't want to leave.

For her own good, Mandi had better grow up.

"Made me dizzy," Mandi complained. She pushed Zack away, rubbed her forehead, then looked me over. "Why don't you get dressed, and we'll go back to the village. That outfit is unbe—unbeliv—just too corny."

Jesse didn't see it that way. "Gwennie looks beautiful."

"Yeah," Roscoe sneered, as Perch bugged his eyes out in the direction of my wet blouse.

In another place I might have flipped him off, but Jill's glance slipped past Jesse. I knew by the way she straightened her shoulders Nana was coming.

"Hello, Mrs. Cook," Jill said. "It's great to see you again."

"Thank you," Nana said, then looking at me, she turned the garland around and around in her hands. "Gwen, you don't really have to watch the embers down, if you'd like to take care of your friends."

I wouldn't like to. I wanted to stay with Jesse.

But Nana looked pointedly at Mandi, whose expression had changed from pouty to ill.

"Are you all right, dear?" Nana asked, but I knew she didn't feel solicitous. My friends were embarrassing her.

I didn't know how Nana was going to smooth this over.

She didn't. To my amazement Nana went to join *her* friends and left mine with me.

"She needs to sit down," Zack said, trying to get out of puking range.

Perhaps as a distraction, Mrs. Leoni began a flute solo. I felt the music curl through Jesse, and Jill must have noticed too, because when a couple of the Hobbit guys sang along to "Greensleeves," so did she, looking right at Jesse.

Jill has an incredible voice. She's going to be big-time, really. She performs the national anthem *a cappella* at school assemblies and sings solos at graduation and football games.

Jesse was charmed, and I hated feeling jealous on top of everything else. The song seemed to last forever, but finally she got her applause and a load of new fans.

"That was wonderful," Jesse told her, and I really hoped Jill's voice was what people remembered in the morning instead of Mandi's moan.

Sitting next to the bonfire, head between her knees,

Mandi said, "I think I'm going to be sick. I wanna go to bed now."

No surprise, Zack and his crew were moving down the beach, away from us and toward the highway, without a good-bye.

I wasn't ready to leave. It was Midsummer's Eve, and I was the Queen!

"We're supposed to stay up all night," I said, but my voice sounded weak.

"Stay with me," Jesse whispered into my neck. My stomach flip-flopped and I shot Jill a pleading look.

"Your house was open," Jill said at last. "C'mon, Mandi."

Jill hauled Mandi up by her arm, but it was me Mandi reached toward.

"Gwen! God, you can see him later." Her hot-pink lipstick was gooey, and her breasts were about to spill out of her top. I wanted to slap her. When she added, "We're only here for a little while, and we're your real friends," I almost did.

"Shut up, Mandi," I told her.

She started to cry, and Jill's eyebrows shot up. Jesse didn't say a word.

"Well look at her," I tried to excuse my harshness. "She's—"

Jill held her hands up in surrender.

"I didn't say anything," she told me, but I didn't

need Jesse to read her eyes for me.

They'd driven all the way up here to see me. What kind of friend would ignore them to be with a guy she'd only known for a few days?

Even if he cared more about me, even if we were the Summer King and Queen, even if I loved him.

"I'd better go," I told him.

Alarm flared in his eyes.

"Jesse, what?" I whispered. Anger wouldn't have surprised me, or even sadness, but he looked as if I'd given up our very last night together.

"I'm not, am I?"

My god, I was asking him to read my mind. I was really losing it.

Jesse didn't answer. He looked down the beach the way Zack and his crew had gone, thinking, I supposed, that he didn't have to walk me home with them out of the way.

"I'll stay here," he said, then squeezed my arm and returned to the bonfire, where Sadie Linnet was passing a platter of fresh shrimp.

"Is he mad at you?" Jill asked as we walked.

"I don't think so," I told her. "He doesn't get mad."

"Ha!" Mandi said, looking after him. "Don't you believe it. He's sizing up that bimbo right now."

"He's not either," Jill said in a singsong voice as we started up the beach toward my cottage.

Just the same, I couldn't help looking back to see if he was talking to that girl.

I recognized her then. It was Jade, from the dark side street, one of Zack's friends, and I was walking away, leaving her alone with Jesse.

At three thirty in the morning I was sprawled on my couch, eating pizza I didn't want, with guests I didn't welcome. Even Gumbo had found someplace to hide.

"It's your favorite," Mandi said, rejuvenated by the pineapple and jalapeno cheese pizza. They'd brought it with them. "After all that codger food at the Inn, we knew you'd be dying for something from Rico's."

There was no reason that should have made me mad, but it did. Nana and Thelma made great food. Gourmet food.

"You pretty crazy about that guy?" Mandi asked while she stared into my refrigerator. Looking for something else to settle her stomach, I guess.

"His name's Jesse," I corrected her. I know I didn't snarl or anything, so why did they give each other that look?

"Sor-ree," Mandi snapped.

Usually I would have apologized, but not this time.

"How long have you known him?" Jill asked.

What was this? She knew exactly how long I'd been at Mirage Beach. Less than a week.

My irritation must have shown, because she added, "I just meant, did you know him when you lived here before?"

I laughed. "Sort of, but not very well."

"So, I guess things got intense in a hurry."

"Yeah," I said, but I really don't think she understood. Otherwise, wouldn't she have been happy for me?

"Hey!" Mandi said. She gulped a carton of orange juice and wiped her lips. "You know what we're gonna do?" Mandi crossed the room and pushed aside two sleeping bags she and Jill had piled in the corner. She unzipped a duffel bag. "I brought all my stuff to do a makeover on you, so tomorrow at your village festival thing, you'll look totally hot."

"Mandi, I don't think Gwen feels like having a makeover in the middle of the night."

Thank you, I mouthed at her.

"Of course she does." Mandi started piling white tubes, plastic gloves, and a clutter of brushes on my kitchen table. "Go wash your hair."

I went because I was shivering and cold, and I really hoped they'd both be asleep when I got out of the shower. If they were, I'd sneak out and find Jesse.

I didn't close the bathroom door completely, in case they wanted to ask me where something was. To be fair, I was being as terrible a hostess as they were being bad guests.

I could hear them talking. Mostly Mandi, because even though she'd pulled herself together, she was still tipsy and talking too loud. Mad as I was, I was so glad I hadn't left her with Zack.

"You know, I always thought I'd be the one to fall in love at first sight," she said.

Jill grumbled something sarcastic, but I guess that was the end of it, because Mandi began babbling about finding the right hairbrushes. I figured I wouldn't miss anything if I climbed into the shower, but I did feel ridiculously bad about sudsing the Midsummer Eve seawater out of my hair.

I was rubbing off with a towel when I heard Mandi again. "Do you think she got together with him so soon to give people something else to talk about?"

"Instead of that night?" Jill asked.

I'd told Jill about the sleepwalking and Dr. Cates. Only Jill, because I didn't think I could trust Mandi not to tell. Apparently I couldn't trust Jill, either.

It was *my* secret. She had no right to tell, and she'd sworn, under pain of death, to tell no one. It was just between us.

Well, I guess not. I jerked on fresh jeans and a sweatshirt. I wrapped a towel around my hair, and the minute I walked back into the kitchen, Mandi snatched the towel off. "I'm going to streak it blond like mine," she said, mixing silver paste in one of my coffee mugs.

Betrayal and the bleachy smell made me sick.

"It's really ironic," I said to Jill, "that my parents left Mirage Beach because it was a gossipy little town, and you, sitting in Valencia, couldn't keep my secret even a week."

They had the decency to look chagrined that I'd overheard them.

Jill sat down at my table and matched her fingertips together in this calm, meditative manner. "Gwen, don't take this the wrong way, but it's also only been one week that you've known this guy."

"So what?" I said. "He's amazing. Why can't you be glad for me—"

"You almost went off with him instead of us," Mandi said.

I looked at Jill and she nodded.

"Is that what this is about?" I asked. "You're jealous?"

They both started saying, no, that wasn't it at all, but that's what it came down to.

"But I did leave Jesse," I said, finally. "And I did it for you, Mandi, because Zack is bad news."

I was about to tell her he was a sadistic thug and that she should be mature enough to see that, but then Mandi sort of smirked, and I lost my desire to lecture her. Why should I care, if she didn't?

"I think we should all go to bed," I said, finally.

"That would be best. We'll all feel better in the morning," Jill said. She made a smoothing motion with her hands.

Jill always knew best. Just ask her. I wondered why I'd never noticed it before. I knew these two were my friends, but right now, I couldn't remember why.

Mandi was crying again. "I wish I was sober enough to drive home."

"Well, you're not," Jill said, slipping into her sleeping bag. "And besides, it's my car."

I trotted upstairs to my loft and tried to sleep, but I couldn't. And since I didn't get undressed and put on a nightgown, I guess I never really wanted to. If Gumbo had been there, curled up beside me, I might have lasted longer. But the smell of the sea wafted through the skylight. I had to find Jesse. Together we'd watch the sun rise on Midsummer morning, just the way I'd planned.

WILD WESTERN THIMBLEBERRY
(Rubus parviflorus)

◈

*V*elvety pink berries, dark green leaves, and cautioning spines mark *this woodsy berry. Cousin to the blackberry, it may live at the shore, in red-wood forests, and on the High Sierra, but deprived of moisture, it will sicken and die. Thimbleberry wine is nectar to fairies, and herbal lore praises the thimbleberry for shielding the virtuous. Running through a thimbleberry thicket is rumored to dispel illness, while a sip of thimbleberry tea returns evil to those who wish it on others.*

CHAPTER THIRTEEN

◈

I couldn't find Jesse.

First I checked the bonfires. Smoke sat heavy on the early air, and I wondered if I should take it as an omen.

A few people were still watching the fires die down. Red O'Malley sat upright, a gray-striped blanket around his shoulders, while Shannon, Eric, and their three little boys slept. Hearing me, Red looked away from the white twists of smoke and raised a hand in greeting.

I'd finally remembered what it was I liked about him. That night on the beach, he'd been the first person to reach me. I didn't know if he'd been a volunteer fireman, if he'd been working with the sheriff, or what. I did know he'd swept me up from the sand and without asking a single question, taken me to my mother.

Now his smile came from one insider to another. That was all about being crowned, I thought.

Leaving the bonfires last night had been a mistake. I wished I was still wearing rumpled leggings and my crown. And I wished Jesse were walking beside me. But I returned Red's smile, knowing I'd still won something that would make me a permanent part of Mirage Beach.

I tiptoed past the sleeping family to the bonfire Jesse and I had leapt. It had burned out long since. Gray ash stirred in the early breeze, whispering secrets I was too dense to understand.

Next I went down to the cove. It was silent except for wavelets, searching the sand for the seals who'd fled the noise and had yet to return. Nana said the cows and their young would come back this evening and sleep so soundly we wouldn't hear them for several days.

Last I went to Little Beach, stopping atop the highest dune. The beach was littered with skeins of kelp and driftwood. A few pieces were black, probably washed in from a bonfire. Jesse wasn't there, either.

I sat cross-legged, watching the tide roll in from a pewter and pink sky. Gulls banked and cried, scolding me for not observing at least one Midsummer morn tradition. I was Queen, after all.

I built a cairn of rocks, about a foot high, and topped it with some tiny purple flowers. Probably it was an offering to fairies or summer spirits. I really didn't know, but I felt better for doing it.

Standing, I looked back at my cottage. Jill and Mandi wouldn't be up for hours so I had no excuse to skip work. Would Nana have her dark tea today or was that tomorrow?

No matter, I thought. I'd feel better helping over there. The Whartons would be awake and eager for breakfast, even if the Hobbits slept in.

Tired and melancholy, I still picked up the pace a little, excited that I'd won a crown. The Whartons, who'd admired Jesse and me together, would be pleased, and that was good for business. Besides, I still believed I'd see Jesse, soon.

Thelma greeted me as befitted royalty.

"Morning, your Ladyship," she joked, and my gloominess didn't keep me from making a curtsy. "Hear you had an early evening," Thelma said, checking the eggs she was coddling before giving a small kettle of hollandaise sauce a stir.

"Not really," I said. I found the biggest mug in the cabinet and poured myself a cup of black coffee. "My friends kept me up late," I said, drizzling in a little milk.

I sipped with my eyes closed, and only when I opened them did I notice Nana was sitting at the kitchen table with her leg elevated.

It sure hadn't taken me long to forget why I was

here. Nana needed my help. I bent to kiss her cheek.

"Why don't you slip off to bed and let me take over," I asked her.

Thelma hmphed, indicating she'd already tried that tactic, in vain.

"And let you girls have first crack at the eggs Benedict? I hardly think so," Nana said. "What I would appreciate though, is if you'd slip a full-length apron on over those jeans."

I'd totally forgotten what I was wearing. Before I could apologize, Nana had left for the parlor.

While Nana dined with the Whartons, I came back into the kitchen for a second cup of coffee.

"I've been wanting to ask you something," Thelma said.

"Okay," I said, bracing myself.

"Seeing you last night around that Zack McCracken, I noticed how he can't seem to decide if he likes you or hates you."

"He hates me," I said. "Neither of us is confused about that."

"I wouldn't be so sure," Thelma told me. "He may hate you because you won't give him the time of day— not that you should."

I think it was exhaustion, not patience, that made me wait for Thelma to go on.

"Well, has he bothered you up at the cottage?"

"No—" I began, then stopped. There'd been the wet footprint. And the feeling I was being watched, but surely those were paranoia. "Why are you asking?"

I was getting chills, even in this kitchen, warm from baking.

"A few months back I caught him in the cottage. Said he was coming up there to shave and take a shower, even though we had the power turned off, so there was no hot water."

I thought of the razor and the missing key, but I didn't say anything. I thought of the way he'd grimaced when I sat on the dirty pier beside Jesse.

"It's admirable that he wants to be clean—" I began, but Thelma cut me off.

"But no excuse for burglary."

"Right," I said, "and I don't think he can get in. I set the dead bolt every night, and my dad checked the place out pretty thoroughly."

A bell tinkled from the parlor. Thelma swatted the seat of my jeans.

"That should never happen!" she scolded.

"I know," I said, and bolted out of her reach.

It was eleven o'clock by the time I returned to my cottage.

I'd already slipped past my hedge and said good morning to my spider, when I turned back and picked three blackberries. Most of them were dark purple now, instead of green, but they were still hard when I squeezed them.

I gave them an experimental chew, just the same. Still pretty darn tart, but better. I shuddered a little at the taste and glanced up in time to see a half-feathered nestling coast from the swallow's nest to the far end of the hedge.

The mother bird swooped after him, scolding, I thought, or lecturing about self-preservation and the presence of humans.

And cats, I thought, as I entered my dark cottage.

Mandi and Jill were still asleep and there was no sign of Gumbo.

Even when I put fresh food in her dish, she didn't appear. I jogged upstairs to see if she was sleeping in her favorite sunbeam on my bed. She wasn't.

"Gumbo? Here kitty, kitty?" I listened. Nothing.

Last night I'd left the cottage open for Jill and Mandi. They'd dropped off their suitcases and sleeping bags. My breath caught. Had they stopped here before going to Siena Bay? Or after, with Zack and his crew? Had Zack been inside my house? .

I ran back down the stairs, calling more loudly. "Gumbo!"

Jill sat up, rubbing her eyes. Mandi rolled on her side and opened her mouth experimentally. Then very slowly, she sat up too.

"What's happening?" Jill asked.

"I can't find Gumbo. Was she here when you came in last night?"

"I didn't see her," Jill said. "But you know how she hides from strangers." Jill blushed; last night's fight must have rushed back to her. From the quick glance she shot at Mandi, I knew they hadn't arrived alone.

"Mandi, did you see Gumbo?"

"God, Gwen!" Mandi shielded her eyes from daylight as I pushed back the gauzy curtains. "You told me not to let her out and I didn't."

Mandi held a pillow over her face, and for one minute, I really hated her.

Gumbo had been outside before, but not at Mirage Beach.

I took a deep breath. All I could do was get Mandi and Jill out of here and hope Gumbo returned.

"We've missed the Midsummer Madness parade," I said. "If you want to see any of the events in town, we should probably get going."

"We'll take two cars," Jill said, standing and stretching. "You'll probably want to stay longer than we can."

"If I don't get some aspirin, I'll die," Mandi said. "That guy tried to poison me."

Jill and I shot Mandi the same accusing look.

"Well, he did," she mumbled, and wobbled to her feet, still holding her head. We made it out of the cottage in about twenty minutes, with Mandi vowing she didn't care how she looked, although she had spent eighteen of those minutes monopolizing the bathroom mirror, stroking on mascara, with her cell phone clamped between her ear and shoulder, complaining because Cook's Cottage had such terrible reception.

By the time we arrived at the village, Midsummer Madness was in full swing. Shops were decorated with balloons, pennants, and SALE! signs.

We bought mochas and sipped them as we walked around. Though I wanted to check out the traditional Siena Bay Fisherman's Faire—with old-fashioned games, a rag doll booth, and blackberry shortcake concession—I tagged along with Mandi and Jill, looking in shop windows.

It was only for another hour. After that I had to find Gumbo. And Jesse.

We walked by the Bling Bling video arcade, loud with its hooting games. It was crowded with kids.

Mandi peered in through her sunglasses, then shook her head. She wasn't finding much to like in Siena Bay.

"This cobblestone effect is cool," Jill said, looking down at the grass-bracketed rocks in front of a rustic office building I recognized from my last trip to Siena Bay.

One of the signs read, DR. JACK CATES, CHILD AND FAMILY THERAPIST. Jill came to a dead stop.

"I know I screwed up big-time telling your secret," Jill began.

"And it wasn't last week," Mandi said.

Jill looked at her, aghast.

"Well, it wasn't," Mandi said, pushing her sunglasses farther up her nose. "Jill knew she could trust me to keep quiet, and I did."

"So, it's you I can't trust?" I asked Jill. My tone was probably kind of ironic, since Jill always acted like she knew what was best for everyone.

"You can, but—" Jill pursed her lips in this disapproving way. "I'm not perfect, you know."

"Who said you were?" I snapped. "You weren't even happy for me about Jesse."

"We told you—" Jill began.

"No. Oh, no. You guys told me you thought I'd go off with him, but I didn't. I didn't choose him over you!" I shouted, making a mother walking past glance at us. "So, really, why aren't you excited for me?"

"Well, if you hadn't noticed, I'm too busy to have a social life," Jill said, putting a hand on one hip.

"So what?" I asked. "So I can't have a boyfriend? And what about you?" I asked Mandi. "Jesse is absolutely the fairy-tale kind of guy you drool over. And we were crowned King and Queen! Why aren't you just"—I searched for a word—"ecstatic?"

"Well, if it were me, I would be," Mandi admitted quietly.

"Then stop settling for losers," Jill said, nudging her.

"She's right," I rushed in.

"Look, those kind of guys are attracted to me," she said. "I can't help it."

"You can help it," I told her. "You've got more going for you—"

"And you—" Jill interrupted, turning on me again.

"Yeah," I said, throwing my empty cup into a trash can with way too much energy. "What?"

"I *am* sorry," Jill said, sounding sincere. "I'm glad you've got a boyfriend who's kind of," she shrugged, "out there."

"Gee, thanks," I said.

"No, I mean it. It's a step in the right direction. You've always tried too hard to fit in and be unexceptional—"

My jaw dropped. It really did.

"You don't want this fight to be over, do you?" I asked.

"Gwen," Mandi said. "She's kind of right. Like, you quit diving when you were getting really good and could have won the state championship. What was that about?"

"Not—not that I didn't want to stand out," I insisted. "And I wasn't going to be state champion."

"How do you know?" Jill demanded.

"Because I wasn't brave enough," I said, knowing it was the truth. "You have to do harder and higher and—"

They started disagreeing. Loudly. But I could hardly

hear them. Suddenly I thought of Mirage Point. I shook my head, as if I could get rid of the image.

"So maybe we should all go see the shrink," Mandi mused, slinging an arm around my shoulder. "We're underachievers and Jill's an overachiever. Yeah? Is that what you're saying?" she asked Jill.

"I don't know anything," Jill said. "Except I'm just sorry."

I looked down at a crack in the cobblestones where a weed had sent up a pale green shoot. "Circle of arms, circle of strife, circle of blooms, circle of life." Maybe the Celts had nailed it a thousand years ago. Maybe life was that simple: friends, fights and flowers. You got past the hurt and kept going. Except for the sounds of the fair and the swish of tires as a guy in a flashy bike jersey pedaled past.

I looked up as Jill reached for my hand. I took it.

"I really am sorry. You can trust me," Jill apologized again.

I squeezed her hand as Mandi grabbed my other one.

"And me," Mandi said. "I *can* keep a secret. You just have to, you know, hold me by the ears and stare into my eyes and make sure I understand."

"Mandi," Jill said in a cautioning tone and our clasped hands loosened.

"I know, I know, but low self-esteem works for me

as a, you know—humor thing," Mandi said.

"Okay," Jill and I said together then we gave our hands a last squeeze, released, and suddenly I was pretty sure this was something the three of us would get over.

I was sure of it when Mandi grabbed Jill's arm to drag her back toward the car, but not before sticking out her tongue and saying to me, "Now witch, go find your King of Whatever and have your happily ever after. And when we see you again? Don't spare the details!"

I knew something was wrong when I turned off the highway and onto my road.

Jesse was running right toward me. He was wet and bare chested, and his face was set in a high-anxiety frown.

I shoved open the driver's door and got out.

A screaming screech sound stopped me.

"What is it?" I shouted at him, but I knew. That scream was Gumbo's.

"I'm sorry," he shouted at me, over his shoulder. Then he was running to my cottage.

A brown fishing net was suspended over my front door. It jounced and swung, full of a furious and terrified Gumbo. How long had she been there? What had been done to my cat while I'd been strolling and talking with my friends?

I barely noticed the swallows' nest shattered all over the deck, as I struggled to figure out how to get Gumbo down.

If Jesse hadn't been there, I would have dragged a chair from the kitchen table. The net was fastened to the porch rafters, seven feet high, but he jumped up and snagged the fastening.

"Don't let her loose out here!" I warned.

The look he flashed me would have been terrifying if I hadn't been focused on Gumbo. "She'll run away."

"She likes me," he managed, as a claw barely missed his cheek.

"She doesn't like anyone now," I said.

"Don't tell me what it's like to be in a net. Just get the door open and watch out!"

I did, and as soon as he'd wrestled the net and Gumbo inside, I ran around checking windows so that she couldn't escape.

I was upstairs when I heard Gumbo's first frantic circuit of the living room. Something fell and broke on the wooden floor. Then there was silence.

"She got herself free," Jesse shouted up to me.

"Is she okay?" I asked, but Jesse didn't answer. He kicked the empty net toward the door with more hatred than I'd ever seen directed toward an inanimate object. "It was Zack, wasn't it?"

"Can't you smell it?" Jesse's face was brown-red with

258

fury. I wasn't sure what he meant. But I knew Zack had been in my house. Zack hated me for some reason. Maybe he'd never forgiven me for helping him when he couldn't help himself.

Thelma had warned that helpless creatures weren't safe around Zack McCracken, and he'd just proven it. Gumbo was lucky to be alive.

"He's got to stop this," Jesse said.

I noticed the sunrise shell, broken on the floor. In her wild escape Gumbo had knocked it off the table. I picked up both halves and set them back where they belonged.

"Do you want to come with me to talk with him?" I knew I wouldn't have much effect on Zack, alone. "I bet he's working at the video arcade."

I picked up my car keys and Jesse hurried after me, but I could tell something else was wrong.

"What?" I asked him, and then wanted, more than anything, to take it back. Jesse looked scared. I touched his cheek. "Don't go with me if—"

"It's cars I'm afraid of, not Zack. But if I swim, there may not be time. That's all." He tossed his drying hair back from his eyes.

"I'm a pretty good driver."

"All right," he said, but I had to open the passenger door for him and fasten his seat belt. Even then, he said, "It's a very little car."

When I turned the key in the ignition, before I even

put the Bug into reverse, he grabbed the window frame with one hand and the emergency brake with the other.

"I need to release this," I told him cautiously. "And don't jerk it back on or you'll make us crash."

Jesse nodded. When the car lurched and bumped away from the cottage, much rougher than usual, he crossed his arms over his bare chest. His eyes stayed closed all the way to Siena Bay.

The Bling Bling video arcade was dim. From what I could see, it was sort of a retro place, not like the mall arcades in Valencia. Instead of joystick and push-button games, there was pinball and stuff like that, and it was too dark for a bright June day.

I was trying to decide what to say, when Zack spotted us.

"He's got to stop this," Jesse said again.

Still wearing his wine-stained T-shirt, Zack squared off, making sure Perch and Roscoe, loitering nearby, saw us coming. He signaled for them to follow, but Roscoe hung back.

Zack turned and snarled something at him. I couldn't hear what, but I heard Roscoe's reply.

"I seen that guy fight before."

Perch hesitated too, and his weakness infuriated Zack. "Stay back with the babies, then." He pushed Perch into a group of little kids who'd turned to gawk.

Then Zack came toward us.

"Well, look what the cat dragged in," he said, and guffawed.

Jesse closed the distance between them with a step so quick, all Zack could do was get his hand up and shove Jesse's chest.

Jesse stood firm.

"You really scared that cat," Jesse said quietly, but there was menace in his tone.

Zack used both hands to shove Jesse again.

"I see you brought your little Summer Queen to cry, so I won't hurt you too bad," Zack taunted.

I gasped as Zack threw a punch, but Jesse leaned to one side, dodging Zack's fist so that the swing looked big and clumsy.

"Wow! Cool!" A kid cheered as, behind him, two warriors battled endlessly on a screen.

Zack and Jesse ignored everything but each other.

"Just say you'll stop hurting things," Jesse told him. Zack lurched at him again, and this time Jesse grabbed Zack's arm and pulled him off balance, sending him headlong into a flashing video game.

"You guys!" I yelled, but it was way too late.

Zack was fighting scared, but Roscoe and Perch didn't see it. They cheered him on as, blond hair flapping, Zack threw himself at Jesse. This time Jesse didn't step away. With a sound like a growl, he rammed his shoulder into Zack's, slamming him against another video game.

Face down, Zack's feet slipped, and blood smeared the floor as he tried to get up. He lifted his mouth clear enough to say, "Those seals are so dead!"

I expected Jesse to attack him then, but he knew Zack was beaten. Now he made sure Zack knew, by not letting him up. While he held one palm in the middle of Zack's back, Jesse talked adamantly.

I couldn't hear what he said, but while I strained to listen, I heard someone calling my name.

"Gwendolyn?" Mr. Wharton squinted into the dark arcade. "Is that you?"

If Nana heard about this—

Jesse had taught Zack a lesson. Everything should have been okay, but this wasn't one of Mandi's fairy tales. Jesse would pay for doing what was right, and so would the sea lions.

But Mr. Wharton was calling me again.

Nana, I thought, remembering how weak she'd looked this morning.

The banging and slamming in the video arcade had stopped, but I could still hear Jesse talking as I rushed out into the sunlit street.

"Mr. Wharton, is anything wrong?"

"I wouldn't say that precisely, but your grandmother told us that if we saw you in the village, we were to let you know she could use your help with tea this afternoon."

"Of course," I said.

"But to tell you the truth, Gwendolyn?" Mr. Wharton confided. "I think your grandmother is a little weary after last night."

I looked back at the arcade, then at Mr. Wharton. "Weary?"

"When we left following breakfast, Mrs. Cook had nodded off in the parlor, and she didn't wish us a good day or even seem to hear us leave. Somehow, that strikes me as simply out of character."

I had to go. Jesse could handle this on his own. It didn't sound like Nana could.

MOONSHINE
(Achillea Yarrow)

❖

Beloved by butterflies and bees, this flower is named for the great Greek warrior Achilles. According to myth, this yarrow grew from the rust Achilles scraped from his own spear, and he used it to heal his soldiers' wounds. In love charms, it allows the harvester to glow like a star through the darkness. Strewn across a threshold, it keeps out evil. Covered with fluffy white or brilliant yellow foliage, it is stronger than it looks.

CHAPTER FOURTEEN

❖

My front right tire was flat when I swerved into the driveway in front of Sea Horse Inn ten minutes later. Now I remembered running over the glass on my way here. I guess I'd had a slow leak for days, and though I didn't get a ticket driving home, I deserved one.

I left the Bug at a run, only to collide with Nana as she hurried onto the front porch to meet me.

"Gwendolyn, what's happened?" she asked, steadying my arm.

"Mr. Wharton said you needed me. You were 'weary,' he said. Is your leg all right? Why did you let me leave after breakfast if—"

Nana made a calming motion with her hands. "I'm fine," she said. "I'm simply not used to staying up so late.

How awkward that he thought me debilitated."

Nana looked a little embarrassed, but that was all. My heartbeat slowed and I took a deep breath. I'd left Jesse . . .

"But I certainly need you now that you're here," Nana was saying. "We're having a dark tea; not to be gloomy," she assured me, "but to block out the gloom. The weather report says it will stay clear, but my sea horse never lies."

Above my head the stained-glass oval hanging from the Inn's rafters spun in the breeze, but sunlight struck emerald, gold, and aqua beams from the mosaic, and the sky didn't look at all threatening.

Inside, the curtains were drawn and the candles were lighted. The Hobbits were playing a complex card game in the parlor and were eager to discuss my reign. I curtsied and tried to joke, but I couldn't stop thinking of Jesse.

Zack would have his revenge. I knew it. Didn't Siena Bay have a sheriff? Why hadn't he shown up and locked Zack away?

"We're pretty burned out, too," Arnold said, so I guess he didn't see my expression as queenly. "The car's packed, and we're leaving right after tea."

My car had a flat tire, and I wasn't about to change it in the rain. But maybe the storm would hold off until I got home.

"Last free meal till we reach the dorm." Myra gave me a worn grin.

We put out a huge spread for tea and did it early. I felt confined and oppressed by the drawn curtains. When tea was finished, I pleaded for permission to open them. Nana agreed, grudgingly, and when I pulled them back, I saw why.

Thunder clouds crowded the horizon and wind sent a chair skidding across the patio.

"Thelma, we forgot to get the furniture under cover," Nana said.

"We'll help you, Mrs. Cook," Arnold offered, and all four Hobbits trooped outside with Thelma in the lead.

I stayed inside with Nana.

"This has the look of a serious storm," she said. "We may lose power. It might be best for you to stay."

The clouds had turned almost black. They scudded along so fast I could see them move. Waves towered a glassy gray then hammered the beach.

The Hobbits and Thelma staggered against the wind as they carried the chairs around to the side of the Inn.

"Jesse was going to come over," I told Nana, and I hoped it was true. "I don't know where he'll go in this storm."

"Oh Gwennie, surely—"

"He had a fight with Zack," I told her. "He—Zack— put Gumbo in a fishing net and tied her up and—"

Nana patted my shoulder and gave a deep sigh. "All right, then. But be careful."

As soon as she said it, there was a crash against the front window.

All of us rushed to peer out through the pelting rain. Driven by the wind, an orange-eyed gull had smashed into the casement window. Quite dead, it lay on the patio with its neck broken.

I wore Nana's navy blue slicker home, head bent against the rain.

Please let him be okay, I chanted in my mind. *Please take care of him.*

I tried to believe Zack's threat against the sea lions was only a humiliated boy striking out, and this sudden storm was only the sort that happened all the time. It couldn't be the violent tempest caused by the shedding of a selkie's blood. I'd be a fool to believe such a thing. I had no solid proof Jesse was a selkie, but every tendon and nerve pulled tight in me as if I did.

Hoping no one was watching from the Inn, I ran out on the Point and listened. Wind ripped the hood back from my head, and I closed my eyes, trying to hear past the screeching wind and the rocking squeak of the wooden fence. I walked to the head of the path down to the cove and leaned over, straining to hear.

A sudden gust caught the tail of my slicker and blew me. I slipped, got a slanted view of the path to my right and a rock ahead of me, but I didn't fall. I sat down hard,

SEVEN TEARS INTO THE SEA

slipped a few inches, and closed my eyes. No seals called in panic from down below. Maybe they'd sensed the danger and gone.

I could go home.

I trudged through the near-darkness, slashed by wind and rain, wishing I'd left on the lights. I was almost to the cottage when I heard shouting from the beach.

Wind snatched their words, but I thought I saw Roscoe and Perch. Soaked more than rain could manage, they'd obviously been in a boat. And capsized.

I wanted to burst into my cottage and lock the dead bolt. I didn't want to hear what they were shouting, scared and pale, looking back toward Little Beach as if something was after them.

"Don't go down there!" Roscoe yelled. "He's got his dad's skinning knife. Jesus, he's killing everything!"

My mind stopped.

Killing.

No.

"It capsized our boat—"

"This big-ass seal, then the shark—"

Perch grimaced, on the verge of tears. "It's bleeding all over the beach."

I realized I was holding both sides of my head. Covering my ears or steadying my brain, or both. But I felt detached, as if I hovered above my body, noticing they didn't ask for an ambulance or a ride somewhere.

Not that I could have given them one. My car was at
Nana's with a flat tire. They quit staring at me and ran
for the highway.

"—too late," Roscoe screamed.

The storm took the rest of his words, but I wouldn't
have believed them.

"Jesse!" I screamed as lightning flashed overhead.

I rushed down the driveway. Water lapped over it. I
splashed, slipped, and then stumbled on toward the
sand dunes. My hair was plastered to my head, and I
could barely see past the rain.

Nothing lay bleeding on the beach. Those ugly, awful
liars. I heard my own panting as I ran down the beach,
to the water, drenching myself to the knees as I squinted
to make sure Jesse wasn't there, tossed on the waves.

He'd washed up, farther down the shore.

Naked and bleeding, he lay beside a seal skin that
looked like a length of ruined black velvet.

Oh Jesse. I'd wanted proof, but not like this.

I believe, I believe, I believe it.

Was this some Celtic deity's way of convincing me he
still ruled?

I fell on my knees beside Jesse.

"Gwennie, the shark took Zack. All the blood drew it,
but Zack's dead."

Dizziness threatened. First out of relief. Jesse was
alive. He could talk. For a second I even felt sorry for

Zack, cruel as he'd been. But then I looked down.

"All the blood," Jesse had said. All the blood was his.

Dark red and undiluted by the rain, it ran from a slash across his chest. I pressed both my hands over the wound. They weren't big enough to cover it.

"Gwen, stop. I'm . . . okay."

He was *not* okay.

Could I run to Nana's for her car? Get him to a hospital? What would happen when they tried to type his blood, and God, was there time?

"I'll take you to the cottage," I said. I didn't know how I'd carry him, but I knew I could.

"I can walk," he said. "Take my skin."

Mouth open, rain hammering on my head, I stared at it, half-awed, half-disgusted.

"It's the most important thing, if you want to help me—" he said.

I did. Every muscle fiber I'd ever trained and strained would obey me tonight. I grabbed the skin, wedged my shoulder beneath Jesse's, and we started home.

That night, candles took the place of electricity, and magic replaced medicine. On a blanket thrown on my wooden floor, Jesse told me to link my hands, side by side like the sunrise shell he'd given me, and rub my palms on his wound.

"Like the story," he gasped.

But he'd never finished the story. I didn't know what to do, but I linked my hands together, lowered them on that awful wound, and I tried.

Tears started into his eyes from the pain, and I cried too. I was hurting him, helping him, both at once, and my heart would break if his pain didn't stop.

In only moments, it did. The blood beneath my hands grew less slick, then powdery, until only a bruise remained. I watched the pulse beat in his neck, making sure Jesse only slept.

Denial wouldn't work anymore. My heart had known from the beginning that Jesse was a selkie. My head had been more stubborn, but I was sitting on my floor, next to a man I'd healed with my own hands. A black skin lay beside him. His skin.

I gazed toward my living room window. That fierce storm had softened into a warm summer night as soon as his bleeding had stopped.

I could accept this enchantment or choose to be blind.

I took the afghan off my couch and covered him. My hand stroked his forehead again and again, recording each touch in my fingertips so I could hold the feeling forever.

When Jesse's brown eyes opened, he asked with purely human sarcasm, "*Now* do you believe?"

I silenced him with a kiss.

The kiss lasted. It had to. What if there was never another?

But finally I began searching for explanations only words could give me. Except I couldn't find them. I don't think they existed.

"I believe you're a selkie. And you always have been? Even that night?"

He nodded. "I told you. You called me with your tears."

"But not this time." I thought of the quiet cove, the mother sea lions, and how he'd appeared behind me, basking on a hot rock.

"No," he said.

"Why?"

He took my hand, the hand that had healed him. He didn't hold it like a boyfriend this time. He was restraining me, as if I'd strike out.

"Don't be scared," he said.

"I'm not!"

"You're going to be," he said with a regretful laugh.

I waited, because maybe I wasn't so brave after all.

"We come ashore to mate," he said.

I didn't pull away from him, because that wasn't the scary part. I could tell there was more coming. And it would be worse.

"Jesse?" I knew I had to ask, but I couldn't.

I had to see his face when he answered me.

I settled back on the blanket and touched his smooth golden cheek.

"The rhyme—it's at the center of this, right? That

'mayhap seven years,' what does it mean? What does it *really* mean?"

Not what I think it does, please, Jesse. This time I made him read my eyes.

His head dipped. He kissed the side of my jaw, and then he looked into my eyes.

"It's how often I can come back to you."

He might as well have stabbed me too.

"No," I said. "But if I—if we"—I closed my eyes to say it— "if I'm your mate, then you can stay. Right?"

"No. I can come back," he said.

"No?" I cried as if he'd broken a rule. "I don't believe it. Seven years. That would mean, after this summer, I'd be twenty-four before I saw you again. Then, thirty-one"—I kept counting on my fingers—"thirty-eight, forty-five, fifty-two! Jesse! *Fifty-two.* If we had kids, they'd be grown. I would have wrinkles around my eyes from staring out to sea, watching for you. I could die, and you wouldn't hear of it for years."

A flicker of uncertainty crossed his eyes, and I took it for hope.

"But you don't know. You're not sure, are you?"

"It's the way it will be, Gwen."

"But you haven't done this before," I said as a cold infusion rushed through my veins. "Have you?"

"Never, never!" He held me to his chest. It had been torn and I'd healed it, but what was happening to me couldn't be healed. Even he couldn't stand looking at my eyes.

Please help me. I appealed to God, the universe, anyone, or anything. And Jesse felt it and thought of something.

"I could try to stay," he said. Desperate excitement edged his tone. "Hide my skin. Don't tell me where you put it."

I went still, holding my breath. I thought of those woodcuttings that showed selkie wives staring out to sea. Children clung to their skirts, but the selkie wives turned their longing faces to the waves. Could I do that to Jesse?

Yes, I could, a voice vowed in my head.

He'd offered to stay. I hadn't forced him.

"But I love you." I was crying now for real, and my hands were shaking.

"And so, I'll stay." His chin jerked upward, but even as it did, his eyes took in the ceiling, the walls, the closed door and windows.

I love you.

And so I'll stay.

So simple and so wrong.

I love you, so I'll let you go. I'll let you be who you really are.

That was the right answer. It would poison my life, but it was true.

I came up with excuses, with ways to cope. We could live in a house with a swimming pool. Or on an island.

Our house would have open walls so that the wind could blow through. I'd seen that in pictures of homes in Hawaii.

Before I could speak, Jesse clenched his fists.

"Burn my skin," he demanded. "That way I could never go back."

"Jesse, no." I thought of lions in the zoo—caged.

"But I love you," he said.

Wild celebration should have risen in me. In a way it did, but it made the torture worse.

"Gwen, you must destroy it. Otherwise, I'm too weak." He looked furious as he went on. "I tried it last night. I decided to stay at the fire until dawn, not return to the grotto for my skin, not go into the water until I'd seen you again. And maybe if you'd been there, but you weren't and I gave in."

Just like I "gave in" to breathing when he brought me to the surface after that long underwater kiss?

He had no choice.

"I'll always want to go back, but I want you more."

For now, I thought. In time, he'd hate me.

"If you were going to go," my words came rasping from my throat. "When—?"

"Soon," he said, looking eager and awful, at once. "I'm not sure, but I'll know when it's time."

It was already dark. How long did we have? Weeks? Days? Hours?

He kissed me then, a rough and passionate kiss. He did love me, but if I kept him captive, would I ever again hear him laugh?

Had I heard my favorite laugh in all the world for the last time?

"There's this thing I keep thinking, Jesse. So often, you don't know when it's the last time, and you can't really appreciate—"

"It's for the best, Gwen." He sounded unyielding. "If you knew it was the last time, how could you stand it? If I were holding you for the last time, how could I ever let you go?"

For years I'd practiced not crying. I could make myself stop. So I did.

"We'll try it out tomorrow." I cleared my throat and made my voice sunshiny. "Maybe I'll change my mind. Maybe I'll find a perfect hiding place for your skin, but for now—"

He followed my gaze as I looked at the strange black fur beside him.

"I'll take it down to the grotto," he said, then he tried to joke, too. "If Thelma came over to see how you fared in the storm, it would be just a little bit difficult to explain."

He laughed, but it wasn't his real laugh. He bundled that length of satiny skin under his arm and gave me a kiss on the forehead.

I opened the door for him and heard a fluttering in the blackberry bushes.

"What is it?" Jesse asked.

"The swallows?"

It was actually still light outside. After all, it was Midsummer, the longest day of the year. I squatted and I saw wings.

"Look!" I said. "They didn't die. You know, I saw them making test flights, but I didn't think . . ." I shook my head. "I guess they were almost ready."

"Ready enough," Jesse said, and then he jumped off the deck, to the ground.

He was still naked. Someone might see him. But I refused to waste the time it would take to find him clothes that would fit.

"You've got five minutes to get there and back," I told him. "So, hurry."

Jesse didn't say good-bye.

He ran toward the Inn, then turned left toward the Point.

Before those five minutes were up, I knew he was gone.

I can't say what changed. The waves' crack at their peak sounded just the same. So did their searching whispers as they rushed ashore. The air still smelled of salt and kelp and summer, but I felt a new stillness.

I sat on the step until twilight turned black. Then I

went to find my broken sunrise shell.

Even as I picked up the pieces from the floor, I couldn't blame Gumbo for breaking it. In fact, it wasn't broken.

It's true that the two halves were no longer hinged. They weren't clinging to each other, but each was a cream-colored wing with a rosy flush inside.

I held one half in each hand. If I took this shell across the room or across the universe, and the other one stayed here, they'd still be two halves of a whole, and anyone would know they belonged together.

The selkie dove deep. He banked around a thicket of kelp, arrowing toward Mirage Point. Only when his lungs burned did he burst up with unwavering certainty. He shattered the surface into a million silver drops, aiming for dawn's glimmer, then crashed nose down between the waves.

In the moment spray turned to water, he'd seen her. *Gwen.* He knew she'd waited the night for him, then accepted the truth. He wasn't coming back.

It was dawn as he returned to the surface, shaking droplets to a haze around him.

Gwen balanced on the cliff's edge. Her bathing suit was a defiant red splash against the fog.

Did she hate him or love him? From here he couldn't read her eyes.

He swam back and forth, prowling, anxious, far

enough away that she would not see him if she looked.

Gwen stood straight, resolved. As if she had nothing to lose.

That night seven years ago, he'd watched Gwennie stand straight, arms covering her ears, standing tiptoe in her child's white nightgown. Then she'd changed her mind and walked the path to Little Beach.

Now Gwen was no child.

This time she would leap.

He swam closer, chest moving prowlike through the waves, unable to look away. Over her head, her fingers pointed like the tip of the candle flames that had burned around them last night.

She looked down, trusting herself to read the waves' language. Her knees flexed. A rippling pool shone blue amid foaming waters, and she aimed for it. The balls of her feet launched her up and out. An afterimage of scarlet hung on the air as the sea swallowed her.

My sea. My home. A cruel being would go to her now. But he could not.

Eyes wide, he dove in time to see her arch away from the ocean's floor. Bubbles streamed from her mouth. Her hair fanned, red amber. Her smile was victorious as she kicked toward the surface.

In seven years she might decide sea and shore needn't stay separate after all.

In seven years he would return to wait. And hope.